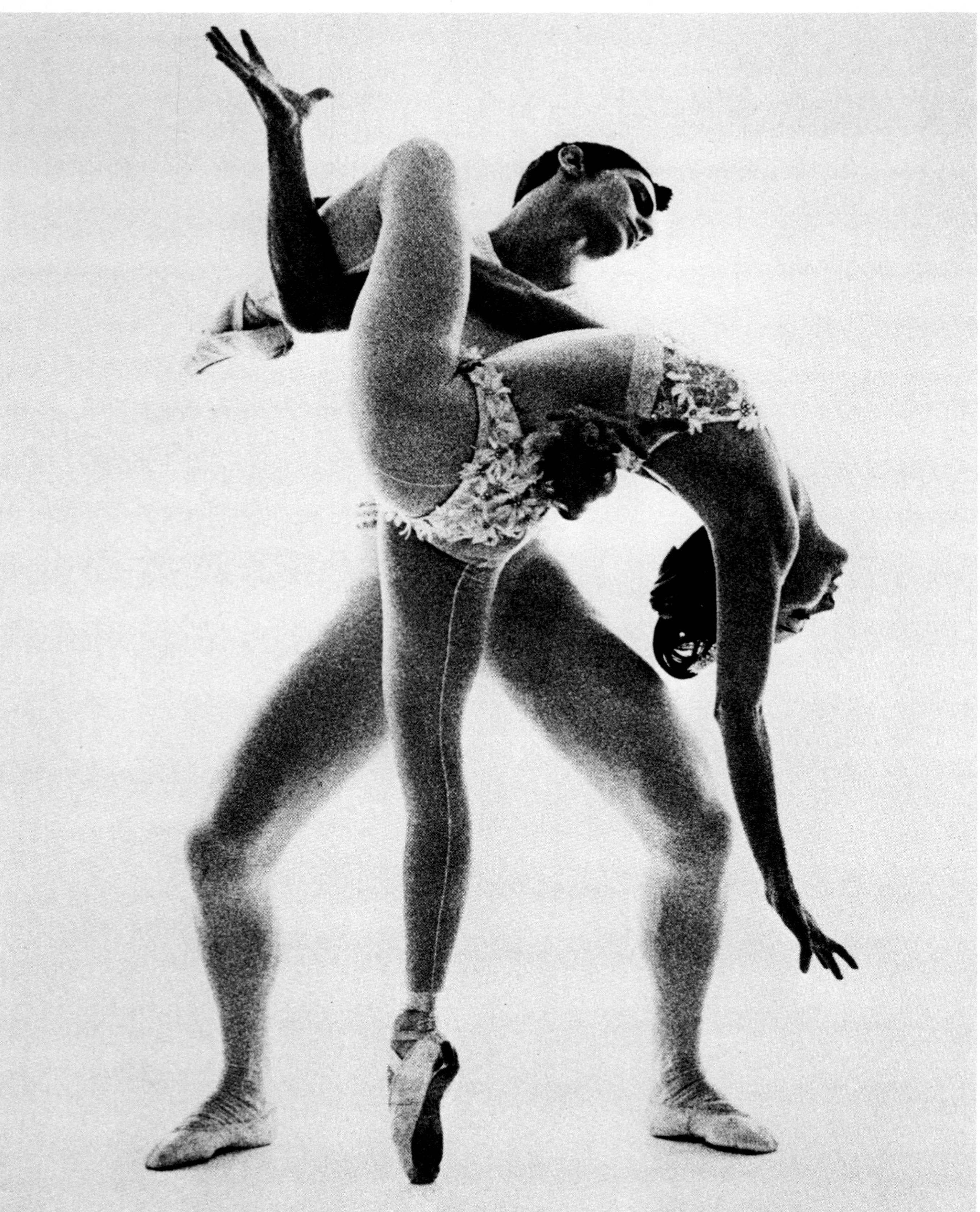

GREAT BALLET STARS
IN HISTORIC PHOTOGRAPHS

248 Portraits of Dancers, 1855 to 1955

Edited by

PARMENIA MIGEL

DOVER PUBLICATIONS, INC., NEW YORK
IN ASSOCIATION WITH
THE STRAVINSKY-DIAGHILEV FOUNDATION

For ALEXANDRA DANILOVA

brilliant ballerina
consummate actress
inspiring teacher
and beloved friend

ACKNOWLEDGMENTS

Dover Publications, the Stravinsky-Diaghilev Foundation and the author gratefully acknowledge the generosity of the photographers who contributed their work and the dancers who provided their portraits. Special thanks are extended to Lynn Garafola, Millicent Hodson, Abbie Relkin, Don Perdue and Norman Crider for their assistance and gifts of photographic material.

Published in Canada by General Publishing Company, Ltd., 30 Lesmill Road, Don Mills, Toronto, Ontario.
Published in the United Kingdom by Constable and Company, Ltd., 10 Orange Street, London WC2H 7EG.

Great Ballet Stars in Historic Photographs: 248 Portraits of Dancers, 1855 to 1955 is a new work, first published by Dover Publications, Inc., in 1985.

Book design by Debby Jay

Manufactured in the United States of America
Dover Publications, Inc., 31 East 2nd Street, Mineola, N.Y. 11501

Library of Congress Cataloging in Publication Data

Main entry under title:

Great ballet stars in historic photographs.
Includes indexes.
1. Ballet dancers—Pictorial works. 2. Ballet—History—Pictorial works.
I. Migel, Parmenia.
GV1785.A1G72 1985 792.8′2′0222 84-21246
ISBN 0-486-24865-8

INTRODUCTION

Ballet dancers have been idols of the public since long before the invention of the camera; originally portrayed in prints and lithographs, they were among the first and most popular subjects of daguerreotypes and carte-de-visite photographs and later inspired many famous camera artists.

Of the thousands of accomplished dancers who appeared in Western Europe, Russia and the Americas, 1855–1955, this selection presents those outstanding for their technical brilliance, their dramatic genius, their physical beauty and elegance and flamboyant personalities. Among them are creators of historic roles and some who had double careers as dancers and choreographers or as founders of leading ballet companies.

Marie Taglioni astounded the audience when she drifted across the stage on the points of her toes. Pierina Legnani dazzled both the public and professionals of her period with her famous 32 fouettés. Cléo de Mérode was known as the most beautiful woman of her era, and doubtless no performer has ever equaled the flights of the legendary Nijinsky or the dramatic range of Leonide Massine.

These and more than two hundred other stars of the ballet galaxy are here depicted in dancing roles and private life, in the great days of their golden youth and the often equally important moments of their mature years.

THE ROMANTIC BALLET

1

2

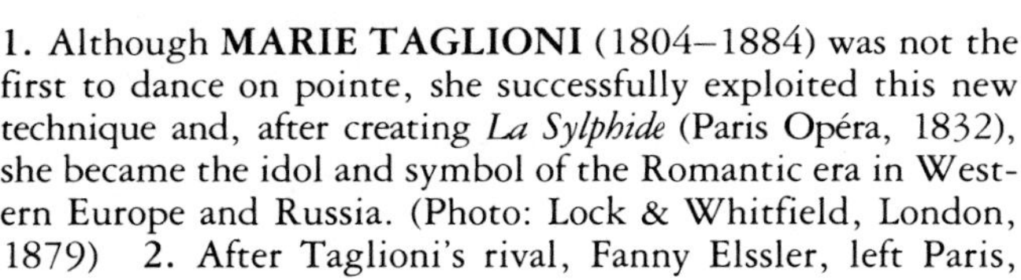

1. Although **MARIE TAGLIONI** (1804–1884) was not the first to dance on pointe, she successfully exploited this new technique and, after creating *La Sylphide* (Paris Opéra, 1832), she became the idol and symbol of the Romantic era in Western Europe and Russia. (Photo: Lock & Whitfield, London, 1879) 2. After Taglioni's rival, Fanny Elssler, left Paris, **CARLOTTA GRISI** (1819–1899), pupil and common-law wife of Jules Perrot, became the next Romantic idol when she created *Giselle* and *La Péri* (Paris Opéra, 1841 and 1843). She was also the lifelong love of the author-critic Théophile Gautier. (Photo: Nadar, Paris, 1865)

3

4

3. FANNY CERRITO (1817–1909) made her first great success in London—in *Alma* (1842), *Ondine* (1843) and *La Vivandière* (1844)—was married to dancer-choreographer Arthur Saint-Léon until 1851 and shared triumphant seasons with him at the Paris Opéra. Along with Taglioni, Grisi and the Danish Lucile Grahn, she starred in Perrot's celebrated *Pas de Quatre* (London, 1845). (Photo: Disdéri, Paris, 1855) 4. "Handsome as Mazilier," said Parisians of **JOSEPH MAZILIER** (Giulio Mazarini, 1801–1868). Taglioni's partner in the original *La Sylphide,* he went on to a long, brilliant career at the Opéra as dancer, choreographer and ballet master. (Photo: Pierre Petit & Trinquart, Paris)

5

6

5 & 6. **MADAME CÉLESTE** (Céline Céleste Keppler, 1811–1882) was one of the first to dance on pointe in the U.S.A. She toured, and was adored by the American public, especially in *The Maid of Cashmere* and as the Wild Arab Boy in *The French Spy* (role in Photo 6). Later she became a successful actress and theater manager in England. (Photo 6: C. D. Fredericks, N.Y.)

7

8

9

7. **JULES PERROT** (1810–1892), an outstanding dancer, partner of Taglioni and also of Grisi, for whom he choreographed solos in *Giselle* (1841) though he was neither credited for it nor danced in that ballet. Unappreciated in Paris, he embarked on a brilliant career in London as choreographer/ballet master: *Ondine* (1843), *La Esmeralda* (1844), *Pas de Quatre* (1845), etc. He then went to Milan (*Faust,* 1848), then to St. Petersburg, where he revived many of his masterpieces and was ballet master until 1858, marrying Capitoline Samovsky. He retired in France, 1859. (Photo: Charles Bergamasco, St. Petersburg) 8. After turbulent years of scandal and intrigue in London, the ravishing Belgian **ADELINE PLUNKETT** (1824–1910), more interested in acquiring lovers than in forging a career, became, in 1845, an étoile of the Paris Opéra and finally a gentle old lady. (Photo: Disdéri, Paris) 9. **CAROLINA ROSATI** (Carolina Galletti, 1826–1905), child prodigy and favorite pupil of Carlo Blasis, appeared at La Scala, 1846, married dancer Francesco Rosati, had triumphant seasons in London from 1847, at the Paris Opéra from 1853 and in St. Petersburg from 1859. In the Russian capital she created Petipa's *La Fille du Pharaon* (1862). Retired at age 36 to Paris and Cannes. (Photo: Mayer & Pierson, London)

10

10. MARIE GUY-STÉPHAN (1818–1873), a leading dancer at the Paris Opéra before going to London, 1841, and then Milan, 1842, and Spain. She appeared with Marius Petipa in Madrid, 1852, and, like him, became expert in Spanish dancing. (Photo: Pierre Petit, Paris, ca. 1861) **11 & 12. AMALIA FERRARIS** (1830–1904), one of the "Seven Pleiades," star pupils of Blasis. Her London seasons, 1850 to 1863, were a success in spite of the decline of the Romantic era. After her Opéra debut in Mazilier's *Les Elfes* (1856), she continued to delight the Parisians until 1863, with interludes in Milan and St. Petersburg. Photo 12 shows her in a revival of the *Pas de Diane*. (Photo 11: Pierre Petit & Trinquart, Paris; Photo 12: Disdéri, Paris)

11

12

13

14

13 & 14. EMMA LIVRY (Emma-Marie Emarot, 1842–1863), the last incarnation of the Romantic ballet, made her Paris debut, 1858, in a revival of *La Sylphide,* seen by Madame Taglioni, who then came out of retirement at Lake Como to teach Livry and choreograph *Le Papillon* (1860) for her. During a rehearsal of *La Muette de Portici,* in November 1862, Livry was fatally burned when her costume caught fire, and she died eight months later at the age of 21. Photo 14 shows her in *Herculanum* (1859). (Photo 13: Disdéri, Paris; Photo 14: Nadar, Paris)

As the Romantic era waned in Western Europe, ballet was in the ascendency in Russia. Inspired by visiting dancers, choreographers and ballet masters such as Taglioni, Elssler, Grisi, Marius Petipa, Perrot and Saint-Léon, Russia was producing its own great performers and creators. Eugenia Sokolova preserved photographs of many of them, including the following and a number of others on later pages. **15. ANNA KOCHEVA** (1840–?), who appeared as the River Congo in Petipa's *La Fille du Pharaon* and as the partner of Lev Ivanov in Saint-Léon's *The Little Humpbacked Horse* (1864). (Photo: Charles Bergamasco, St. Petersburg) **16. ANNA PRIKHOUNOVA** (1830–1887), one of Perrot's favorite dancers. She married Prince Gagarin, a leader of Moscow society. (Photo: Charles Bergamasco, St. Petersburg) **17 & 18. MARIE PETIPA I** (Marie Surovshchikova, 1836–1882). At 18 she became the first wife of Marius Petipa, who noted in his memoirs: "A very graceful dancer whose figure equaled that of Venus." Photo 17 shows her ca. 1860. Associated with the Bolshoi, she had become the corpulent, rather formidable person seen in Photo 18 when she appeared in *Don Quixote,* Moscow (1869). In the same year she was divorced from Petipa, who then married Liubova Leonidovna Savitskaya. (Photo 17: Charles Bergamasco, St. Petersburg; Photo 18: Richard, St. Petersburg)

15

16

17

18

19

20

21

22

19. **MARIUS PETIPA** (1818–1910) in 1869. After appearing as a dancer in Belgium, France, the U.S.A. and Spain, he settled, in 1847, in St. Petersburg, where he danced, staged many revivals and choreographed some 50 ballets, including such masterpieces as *La Bayadère* (1877), *The Sleeping Beauty* (1890), *Cinderella* (1893) and *Swan Lake* (1895), all of them still highly prized and performed everywhere at present. 20. **ARTHUR SAINT-LÉON** (1821–1870) was a great and many-faceted personality of the Romantic and post-Romantic eras—violinist, composer, dancer, choreographer, ballet master, teacher and author of a treatise on dance notation. A brilliant dancer, he appeared in Germany, Brussels, Italy, Vienna and London, where he had leading roles and was married (1845–1851) to Fanny Cerrito. At the Paris Opéra, with Cerrito as dancing partner, he choreographed *La Fille de marbre* (1847), *Le Violin du diable* (1849) and other successes. He followed Perrot as ballet master in St. Petersburg, 1859–1869, choreographing such popular works as *The Little Humpbacked Horse* (1864), and simultaneously was visiting ballet master (under Lucien Petipa, Henri Justament and Louis Mérante) at the Paris Opéra, 1863–1870. He shuttled between Russia and France until his death in 1870, in Paris, where he had just presented his *Coppélia*. (Photo: Disdéri, Paris, ca. 1870) 21. **MARTHA MOURAVIEVA** (1838–1879). The daughter of a serf, this beautiful, raven-haired, lively dancer was a special protégée of Saint-Léon. In 1863 he took her to the Opéra, where her rendition of Giselle was not well received, but in his ballets, in 1864, the Paris public acclaimed her. The wealthy aristocrat whom she married the following year obliged her to give up her career, but she pined for the stage and finally died of consumption. (Photo: H. Laurent) 22. **GIUSEPPINA BOZZACCHI** (1853–1870) was, like Emma Livry, a pupil of the great Paris teacher Madame Dominique (1820–1885). The last sparkling event that recaptured something of the spirit of the Romantic ballet was Bozzacchi's debut at 16 in Saint-Léon's *Coppélia*. Exhausted from overwork and the privations of the siege of Paris, ill with fever and shocked by the death two months earlier of Saint-Léon, Bozzacchi died on the day of her seventeenth birthday. (Photo: A. Liébert, Paris)

LATE NINETEENTH AND EARLY TWENTIETH CENTURIES

23

24

25

23. LOUIS MÉRANTE (1828–1887). Chief ballet master after 1869 at the Paris Opéra, he presided over its dreariest era. Although loved and admired as a performer by his contemporaries, and the choreographer of the successful ballets *Sylvia* (1876), *La Korrigane* (1880) and *Les Deux Pigeons* (1886), he was unable to ward off a period of decadence ill-suited to the splendors of the new opera house inaugurated in 1875. Like the Vestris and Taglioni families, the Mérantes were a dynasty of dancers, including Adelaide,Annette, Dorina, Elisa, Francis, Zina (the Russian ballerina wife of Louis Mérante, Zinaida Josefovna Richard, 1832–1890) and others, scattered in the provinces and Italy. (Photo: Benque, Paris) **24 & 25. MARIE SANLAVILLE** (dates unknown), whose career spanned 25 years at the Opéra, 1864–1869 and 1872–1889. Her portraits and the gallery of buxom ballerinas during the regime of Mérante, himself short and stout, lead us to believe that "amplitude is pulchritude" was his motto. Mlle. Sanlaville, we are told, was especially appealing en travesti. However, she had little competition, as the period produced no male dancers of any distinction, and even Bozzacchi, when she created Coppélia, had a female partner (Eugénie Fiocre, 1845–1908) as Frantz. (Photos: A. Liébert, Paris)

26

27

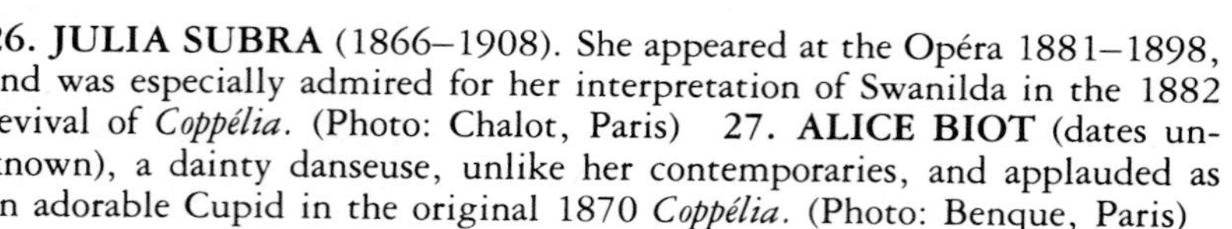

26. **JULIA SUBRA** (1866–1908). She appeared at the Opéra 1881–1898, and was especially admired for her interpretation of Swanilda in the 1882 revival of *Coppélia.* (Photo: Chalot, Paris) 27. **ALICE BIOT** (dates unknown), a dainty danseuse, unlike her contemporaries, and applauded as an adorable Cupid in the original 1870 *Coppélia.* (Photo: Benque, Paris)

28

29

Meanwhile, Italy, though producing no distinguished ballets, was sending forth galaxies of ballerinas, who had reached summits of technical and histrionic achievement. Many went to Russia, where they had a marked and lasting influence, while others appeared in various European capitals and in America. **28. RITA SANGALLI** (1850–1909). After appearing in Italy, Austria and England, she made her American debut at Niblo's Garden, New York, in *The Black Crook* (1866), an extravaganza so successful that in different versions it toured until 1909 and was revived in the 1940s. Mlle. Sangalli arrived to star in *La Source* (1872) in Paris, where she was considered a great beauty, created the lead in many ballets, wrote a book called *Terpsichore* (1875) and married Baron de Saint-Pierre in 1886. **29. MARIE BONFANTI** (1847–1921). A Blasis pupil, she also went to New York to appear in *The Black Crook* and was so delighted with her reception and her American tours that she remained in this country, becoming a successful teacher after she retired. (Photo: J. Gurney and Son, N.Y.)

30

31

32

30. ELENA CORNALBA (dates unknown). In St. Petersburg, Petipa created *La Vestale* (1888) and *The Talisman* (1889) for the Milanese ballerina, but her dazzling triumph was in the role of Electricity in the Paris importation (Eden Theatre) of Luigi Manzotti's extravaganza *Excelsior,* a ballet in 12 tableaux depicting the scientific progress of man. No less electrifying than the star was the line-up of 60 perfectly trained dancers, performing like our present-day Rockettes. (Photo: Newsboy Studios, N.Y.) **31. PIERINA LEGNANI** (1863–1923). She was prima ballerina at La Scala, 1892, and made appearances in Paris, London and Madrid, but her great sensation was in St. Petersburg when she tossed off 32 fouettés in *Cinderella* and *Swan Lake* (1895). She appeared in Russia every year until 1901, and was appointed prima ballerina assoluta, rivaling Kschessinska. **32. VIRGINIA ZUCCHI** (1847–1930) as Esmeralda. A Blasis pupil, who danced in Italy, Germany and London, but had her most brilliant moments in Russia, 1885–1887. A fascinating mime who moved her audience to tears and bravos, she began in St. Petersburg café-concerts in the amusement park, but soon was established at the Imperial Theatre. When she left Russia, she toured briefly and then settled and taught in Monte Carlo. (Photo: Charles Bergamasco, St. Petersburg, 1886)

33 & 34. **CARLOTTA BRIANZA** (1867–1930). Another Blasis pupil, Brianza visited America, 1883, and in 1887 had a triumph in *Excelsior,* imported to Russia. Afterwards, at the Imperial Theatre, she created the role of Princess Aurora in Petipa's *The Sleeping Beauty* (1890; Photo 33), in which ballet she also appeared, aged 54, as the evil and ugly Carabosse in Diaghilev's London production (1921; Photo 34). She taught in Paris and died there. (Photo 33: Edgar de Senoch, St. Petersburg, signed 1892)

35

36

37

38

39

40

35. LEV IVANOV (1834–1901). Brilliant character dancer, who became second ballet master at the Maryinsky and choreographed many successful ballets. In 1892, when Petipa was ill, he took over the choreography of *The Nutcracker,* but his first personal triumph was at the Tchaikowsky Memorial performance, St. Petersburg, 1894, when he restaged Act II of *Swan Lake,* which had been a failure when originally produced in Moscow 17 years earlier. The result was the Petipa-Ivanov collaboration on the splendid complete version at the Maryinsky (1895). **36. MARIE PETIPA II** (1857–1930). The daughter of Marius Petipa and Marie Petipa I, she created many roles in her father's ballets, especially the Lilac Fairy in *The Sleeping Beauty* (1890). She was the common-law wife of the dancer Serge Legat, who committed suicide in 1905 after the Maryinsky dancers went on strike against the directors. Like his more celebrated brother Nikolai, he was a brilliant caricaturist and collaborated on their famous album of ballet portraits. (Photo: Charles Bergamasco, St. Petersburg) **37. ANNA SOBESHANSKAYA** (1842–1918). Leading Moscow ballerina, she created the role of Kitri in the original version of *Don Quixote* (Bolshoi, 1869) and also appeared in the 1877 *Swan Lake* (the photo shows her as Odette). After retiring she became a teacher. (Photo: Scherer & Nabholz, Moscow) **38. PELAGIA KARPAKOVA** (1845–1920). Moscow ballerina, best known for creating the role of Odette in *Swan Lake* (1877).

39 & 40. During and after the Romantic era, August Bournonville (1805–1879) adapted ballets he had seen in Paris or created new ones for Danish consumption, altogether staging some 125 works. After his death, this heritage, much of which is still performed in Denmark and elsewhere, was chiefly preserved by **HANS BECK** (1861–1952). Photo 39 shows this Danish dancer, ballet master and choreographer as he appeared in a revival of Bournonville's *Napoli.* Photo 40 shows him in *Napoli* with **VALBORG GULDBRANDSEN** (née Jørgensen, later Borchsenius, 1872–1948), an important dancer who also helped Hans Beck and later Harald Lander restore old ballets. (Photo 40: Alex Vincent, 1896)

41

41. **ELLEN PRICE DE PLANE** (1878–1968), member of the family of distinguished dancers of English origin, in the title role of Bournonville's version of *La Sylphide* with Gustav Uhlendorff (1875–1928). (Photo: C. St. Eneret, Copenhagen) 42 & 43. **ADELINE GENÉE** (Anina Jensen, 1878–1970). Although born in Denmark, Genée never appeared there except as occasional guest artist under Hans Beck. She performed in Norway and Germany and made tours in the U.S.A., Australia and New Zealand, but the real center of her life was London. There, at the Empire Theatre, 1897–1907, and at the Coliseum after 1911, she became the beloved ballerina who did much to renew British interest in ballet. Entrenched in British hearts, the ballerina became Dame Adeline Genée in 1950, and was also President, 1920–1954, of the institution that became the Royal Academy of Dancing; retired from the stage in 1917. Photo 43 shows her in *Camargo*. (Photo 42: Ralph Dunn, London; Photo 43: Elliott & Fry, London)

42

43

45

44

44 & 45. **ROSITA MAURI** (1849–1923). At long last, the Paris Opéra acquired a brilliant resident ballerina. The vivacious young Spanish dancer, after initial experiences in Barcelona and Milan, performed in Paris from 1878 to 1907 and then taught at the Opéra school until three years before her death.

46

47

46 & 47. CARLOTTA ZAMBELLI (1875–1968). After studying at La Scala, Zambelli began her career at the Paris Opéra, 1894, was promoted to prima ballerina and succeeded to Rosita Mauri. In 1901, she went to St. Petersburg, where she was the last of a long line of Italian étoiles to appear at the Maryinsky. She retired as Opéra performer in 1930, but remained as head of the Opéra school, loved and revered by her associates; also especially admired by British historian Ivor Guest, who wrote a monograph about her. In Photo 46 she is seen in *Javotte* (1909) with Léo Staats (1877–1952), who also choreographed the ballet. (Photo 47: Reutlinger, Paris)

DIAGHILEV AND HIS CONTEMPORARIES

48

49

48–52. VASLAV NIJINSKY (1889–1950). In the spring of 1909, the arrival of Diaghilev's Ballets Russes aroused the blasé Paris public to frenzies of enthusiasm. The technical perfection and acting ability of the performers (there were even virtuoso male dancers!), the opulence, color and exoticism of decors and costumes, the novel music and choreography created a sensation in Western Europe that was constantly renewed until Diaghilev's death 20 years later. Nijinsky, the star performer of Diaghilev's early seasons, had been a prodigy even at his debuts in St. Petersburg. He was the first exciting male dancer to appear in the West since Jules Perrot. A public idol, 1909–1914, in *Schéhérazade* and *Carnaval* (1910), *Le Spectre de la rose* and *Petrouchka* (1911) and many others, he choreographed three ballets of revolutionary novelty: *L'Après-midi d'un faune* (1912), *Jeux* and *Le Sacre du printemps* (1913). After his dismissal by Diaghilev and retirement from the stage, he became mentally unbalanced, 1918, and was never cured. Photo 48, which shows him in his St. Petersburg costume for *Giselle,* was made in Paris, 1910; Photo 49 shows him in *Le Spectre de la rose;* Photo 50, in *Petrouchka;* Photo 51, in *Jeux;* and Photo 52, in *L'Après-midi d'un faune.* See also Photo 78. (Photo 49: E. O. Hoppé, 1911; Photo 50: Bert, Paris, 1912; Photo 51: Gerschel, Paris, 1913; Photo 52: Baron de Meyer, 1912)

50

51

(Nijinsky, *continued*)

52

53

54

53–58. TAMARA KARSAVINA (1885–1978). Nijinsky's most frequent partner won the hearts of Parisians by her dancing and mime, her beauty and charm. Among her most successful interpretations were *Giselle* and *The Firebird* (1910), *Le Spectre de la rose* (1911), *Le Coq d'or* (1914) and *Pulcinella* (1920). After an absence in Russia, she returned to Diaghilev in *Le Tricorne* (1919) in London, where she settled and did much for the progress of English ballet. Author of delightful memoirs, *Theatre Street,* 1930. Photo 53 shows her in St. Petersburg, ca. 1908; Photo 54, in *Giselle;* Photo 55, in *Le Coq d'or;* Photo 56, in *Pulcinella;* Photo 57, as the Miller's Wife in *Le Tricorne;* Photo 58, in *L'Oiseau de feu (The Firebird).* (Photo 57: Malcolm Arbuthnot, London, 1919)

55

56

57

58

(Karsavina, *continued*)

59

59. IDA RUBINSTEIN (1885–1960) as Cléopâtre (1909). She was never a real dancer in the professional sense, but because of her beauty of face and figure and her dramatic personality, she made a great impression in Diaghilev's *Cléopâtre* and the following year in *Schéhérazade*. In 1911, she formed the first of several companies, her private fortune enabling her to hire the leading designers, composers and choreographers, and for 25 years she presented outstanding ballets, always with herself in the central role.

60

60–65. ANNA PAVLOVA (1881–1931). The ideal of both professional dancers and the public, Pavlova was a brilliant star in St. Petersburg before she appeared briefly with Diaghilev in *Le Pavillon d'Armide* and *Les Sylphides* (1909) and *Cléopâtre.* She then formed her own company and toured tirelessly all over Europe, North and South America and Asia until the end of her life. In Photo 60 she is seen in *The Dying Swan.* Choreographed for her in St. Petersburg (1907) by Michel Fokine, it became over the years her most famous role. No ballerina today would appear in a tutu of such stiff tarlatan, so heavily laden with feathers. Pavlova kept many swans at Ivy House, her London residence. The one in Photo 61, Jack, was an affectionate pet. In *Rondino* (1928; Photo 62) Pavlova displayed flirtatious charm. In *La Péri* (1921; Photo 63) in an oriental mood, Pavlova danced with Hubert Stowitts (see Photo 152). Pavlova's chameleon ability to take on the color of the most varied roles is expressed in Photo 64 in the tragic *La Muette de Portici (The Dumb Girl of Portici),* a film produced in California, 1915. Known for her elegance in private life, Pavlova is seen in a 1921 photo (No. 65) in a wrap, perhaps one of those designed for her by Bakst. See also Photo 120. (Photo 60: Hanse Herrman; Photo 61: Lafayette, London; Photo 62: Becker & Maass, Berlin; Photo 63: James Abbé; Photo 64: Eugene Hutchinson)

61

62

63

64

(Pavlova, *continued*)

65

66

67

The "ballet makers" for Diaghilev's first seasons were also dancers. **66 & 67. MICHEL FOKINE** (1880–1942) was a gifted performer and a choreographer of revolutionary ideas in St. Petersburg when he joined Diaghilev. He had been in love with Karsavina, but married the dancer Vera Antonova (1886–1958). Though the Fokines appeared often with the Ballets Russes, Michel, collaborating with the designers Alexandre Benois (1870–1960) and Léon Bakst (1886–1924), was most famous as choreographer of *Polovtsian Dances, Les Sylphides, Cléopâtre, Carnaval, Schéhérazade, The Firebird, Le Spectre de la rose* and *Petrouchka*. After Diaghilev's death, he continued with other companies and founded a school in New York. In Photo 66 he is costumed for a role in *Paquita*. Photo 67 shows him and Vera Fokina at home. (Photo 66: K. A. Fischer, St. Petersburg)

68

69

68. LUBOV TCHERNICHEVA (1890–1976). Wife of Diaghilev's régisseur Grigoriev, who, very proud of her beauty and talent, did everything to promote her career and maintain her high salary with Diaghilev, 1911–1929, and later with Ballet Russe de Monte Carlo and Colonel de Basil's Ballet Russe, during which time her endless amorous escapades (one provoking a duel) caused him great distress. See also Photo 133. (Photo: Mme. S. Georges, London) **69. SERGE GRIGORIEV** (1883–1968) had the formidable task of being régisseur for the Ballets Russes, 1909–1929, and danced in many ballets. He also had the foresight to preserve all the archives—correspondence, bills, contracts, photographs, music, etc.—now in the care of the Stravinsky-Diaghilev Foundation, New York. **70. ENRICO CECCHETTI** (1850–1928) as the Charlatan in *Petrouchka* (1911). Being perhaps the greatest teacher in ballet history did not prevent Cecchetti from enjoying a 65-year career as dancer. He made his debut at age 5 and appeared as the Blue Bird in *The Sleeping Beauty* (1890) and as Carabosse in that ballet (1921). He was ballet master and teacher for Diaghilev's company for ten years.

71

72

The galaxy of dancers brought to Paris by Diaghilev in 1909 included those in Photos 71–81. 71. **VERA KARALLI** (1888–1972), who had the leading role in the preview of *Le Pavillon d'Armide,* also in *Le Festin.* After an interlude as star of the Bolshoi, she returned to Diaghilev, 1919–1920. See also Photo 74. 72. **ADOLPH BOLM** (1884–1951) in *Sadko* (1916). He made his first sensation as the Chief Warrior in *Polovtsian Dances* (1909) and as Pierrot in *Carnaval* (1910). After the Ballets Russes' second American tour, he stayed behind to choreograph at the Metropolitan and Chicago Operas and was a great early promoter of ballet in the U.S.A. (Photo: White, N.Y.)

73

73. **SOPHIE FEDOROVA** (1879–1963) in *A Life for the Tsar,* 1916. She danced in all the ballets of the first Paris season. A star of the Bolshoi, she was later also in Pavlova's company. 74 & 75. **MIKHAIL MORDKIN** (1881–1944). He had been premier danseur in Moscow, and after one year with Diaghilev he left to be Pavlova's partner for her American tour, then was ballet master at the Bolshoi until 1923. He founded his first school and company in New York, 1926, reorganized in 1937 as the Mordkin Ballet, the parent company of Ballet Theatre. In Photo 74 he is seen with Vera Karalli in 1909. (Photo 75: Nickolas Muray, N.Y.)

74

75

76

77

76. LUDMILA SCHOLLAR (1888–1978) in 1909. She graduated from the Imperial Ballet School and a year later joined Diaghilev, was at the Maryinsky, 1917–1921, and then returned to the Ballets Russes with her husband, Anatole Vilzak. After 1925 they shared a teaching career, set up a school in New York and settled in San Francisco. **77. LAURENT NOVIKOFF** (1888–1956). He alternated between Diaghilev, 1909 and 1919–1921, and Pavlova's company, 1911–1914 and 1921–1928. He became ballet master at the Chicago Opera, 1929–1933, and the Metropolitan Opera, 1941–1945. (Photo: E. O. Hoppé)

78

78–81. BRONISLAVA NIJINSKA (1891–1972). She joined Diaghilev with her brother, Vaslav Nijinsky, with whom she worked in Russia to create *L'Après-midi d'un faune* before Diaghilev ever saw this ballet. A fine and conscientious dancer, she became chief choreographer for the Ballets Russes with Stravinsky's *Renard* and *Les Noces* (1922 and 1923), *Les Biches, Les Fâcheux* and *Le Train Bleu* (all 1924). She then choreographed for the Paris Opéra, Opéra Russe à Paris, her own company and many others before settling in California, where she opened a school. She was one of the most original and gifted choreographers of the twentieth century and of equal interest is her autobiography *Early Memoirs,* New York, 1981. In Photo 78 she is seen with her brother in *L'Après-midi* (1912); in Photo 79, as the Humming Bird Fairy in *The Sleeping Princess* (1921); in Photo 80, with Leon Woizikowski in *Le Train Bleu;* in Photo 81, as the Hostess in *Les Biches.* (Photo 81: Georges Detaille, Monte Carlo)

80

81

(Nijinska, *continued*)

82

In 1910, Volinine, Gheltzer and Lopokova added their luster to the Ballets Russes. **82. ALEXANDER VOLININE** (1882–1955) became a premier danseur noble at the Bolshoi immediately upon graduating from the school, 1921. He was Gheltzer's partner in Diaghilev's *Les Orientales* (1910) but left to tour until 1914 with Adeline Genée. Then, for 12 years, he was Pavlova's most famous and enduring partner on world tours. He retired, age 44, to establish one of the best schools in Paris. (Photo: Max Erlanger de Rosen, Paris) **83 & 84. EKATERINA GHELTZER** (1876–1962), also a star at the Bolshoi, appeared only briefly with the Ballets Russes and at the Metropolitan Opera before rounding out her career in Russia until 1930, as highest ranking Soviet dancer.

83

84

85–87. LYDIA LOPOKOVA (1891–1981). She was with Diaghilev, 1910–1929, but with many absences due to her defection to Gertrude Hoffmann's pirated Diaghilev ballets (U.S.A., 1911), to various tours and to numerous love affairs. A dancer of great charm and vivacity, she married British economist John Maynard Keynes and settled in England. **STANISLAS IDZIKOWSKI** (1894–1977), a Polish dancer, unusually small in stature but with brilliant technique and elevation, performed with Diaghilev, 1914–1926 and after 1928, creating many character and classical roles. In Photo 85 Lopokova and Idzikowski are seen in *Carnaval;* in Photo 86 she appears as the Ballerina Doll in *Petrouchka*. (Photos 85 and 87: Count Jean de Strelecki)

85

86

87

88

89

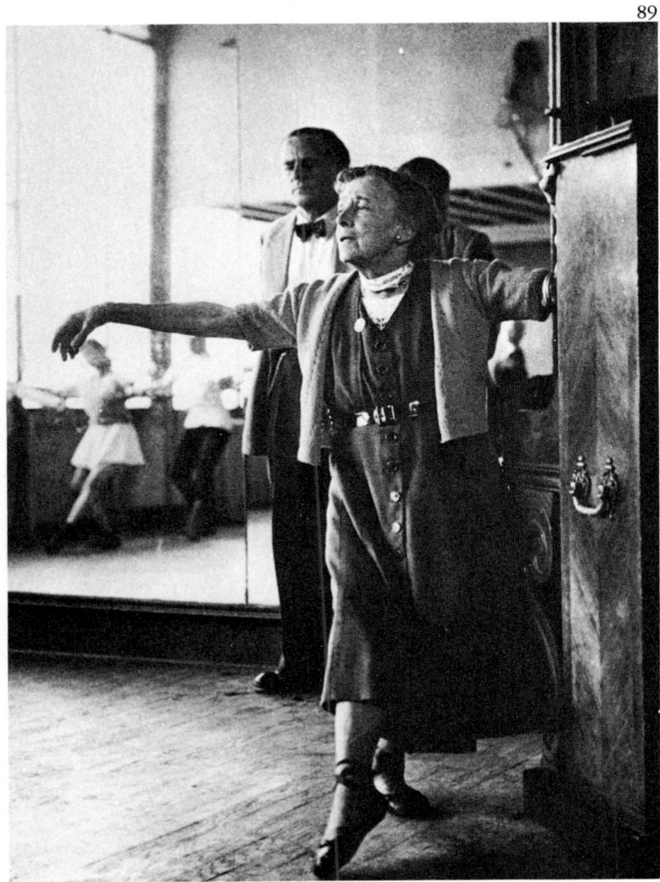

88. ANATOLE BOURMAN (1888–1962), "forgotten man" of the ballet, hardly even mentioned in books on Diaghilev or dance dictionaries. Nijinsky's classmate at the Imperial School, he was from the beginning until at least 1922 with the Ballets Russes, where his wife Léocadia Klementovitch (?–1960) also performed. Author of *The Tragedy of Nijinsky,* London, 1937, a biography which is not at all reliable. **89. OLGA PREOBRAJENSKA** (1870–1962), brilliant prima ballerina of the Maryinsky from 1900, she toured and taught in Russia, Italy, England, Argentina, Germany and the U.S.A., settling in Paris, 1923, as an outstanding teacher. Her one appearance with Diaghilev was in Pavlova's role in *Cléopâtre,* Monte Carlo, 1911. (Photo: Roy Round)

90

91

90 & 91. MATHILDE KSCHESSINSKA (1872–1971). Protégée of the Czar (she later married the Grand Duke André), she had a meteoric career. Prima ballerina assoluta at 23, she was the first Russian to rival the virtuosity of visiting Italians and execute 32 fouettés, and she became a tyrant in St. Petersburg ballet circles. Her long-standing quarrel with Diaghilev was resolved when she appeared for him in *Swan Lake* in London, 1911, with Mischa Elman playing violin accompaniment for her adagio and special solo, and the following year in Vienna and Monte Carlo. Her farewell performance was with the de Basil company, London, 1936. She opened a school in Paris and was still teaching at 90. Author of *Dancing in Petersburg,* New York, 1961. In Photo 91 she is seen with her father **FELIX KSCHESSINSKY** (1823–1905), character dancer of Polish origin, a favorite at the Maryinsky who had appeared as the partner of Marie Petipa I, Paris Opéra, 1862. (Photo 91: Nadar, Paris)

92

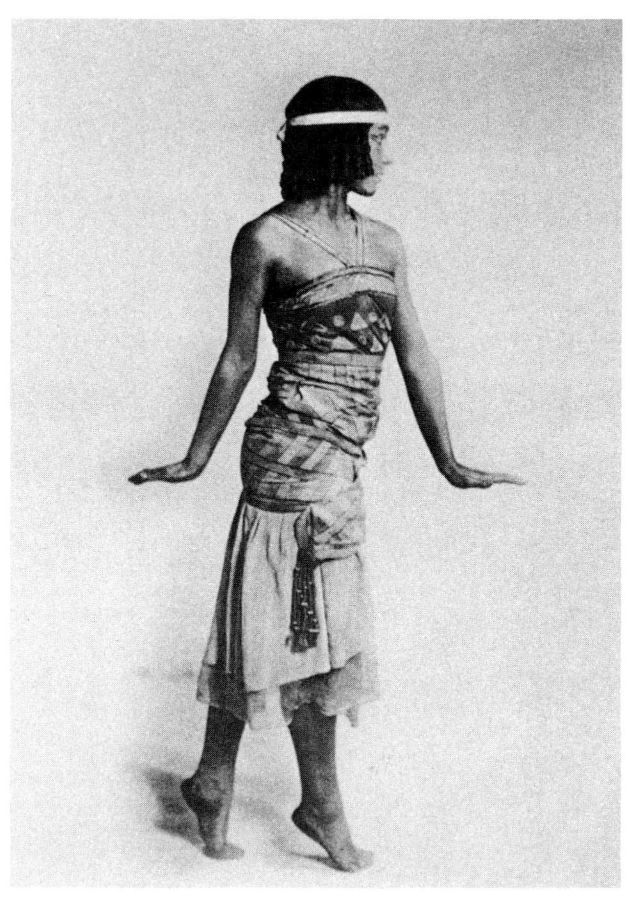

92–94. **LYDIA SOKOLOVA** (Hilda Munnings, 1896–1974). Diaghilev's first English ballerina was with the company from 1913 to 1929, in every sort of role from classical to high comedy, the lead in *Le Tricorne* and (her most famous) the Chosen Maiden in Massine's 1920 revival of *Le Sacre du Printemps*. Author of *Dancing for Diaghilev,* London, 1960. In Photo 92 she is seen in *Cléopâtre;* in Photo 93, as the Apple Woman in *Till Eulenspiegel* (New York, 1916); in Photo 94, in *Daphnis and Chloe.* (Photo 92: White, N.Y., 1916; Photo 93: Ira Hill; Photo 94: Georges Detaille, Monte Carlo)

93

94

95

96

95. LYDIA BONI (dates unknown) as one of the Adolescents in *Le Sacre du Printemps,* the ballet that was the scandal of the 1913 season—decor by Nicholas Roerich, music by Igor Stravinsky, choreography by Vaslav Nijinsky. **96. MARIE RAMBERT** (Cyvia Rambam, then Miriam Ramberg, 1888–1982), Polish dancer, was working with Emile Jaques-Dalcroze when Diaghilev hired her, 1913, to help with Stravinsky's complicated rhythms in *Le Sacre du Printemps.* She also danced in the corps de ballet but soon left to settle in London. She opened a school there, 1920, which produced the finest dancers and choreographers, founded her own company (which still exists) and was one of the greatest influences on British classical and modern ballet. Author of *Quicksilver,* London, 1972. (Photo: Niki Ekstrom, N.Y., 1979)

97

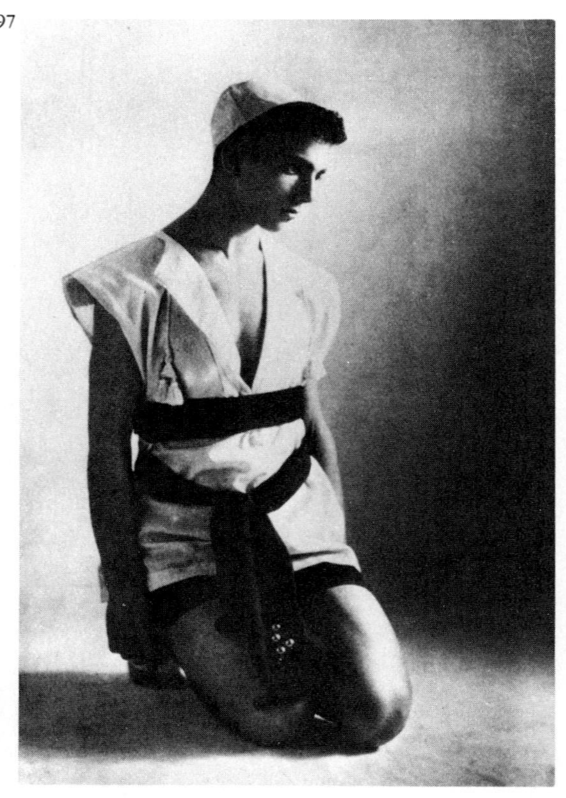

97–102. From Moscow, in 1914, Diaghilev brought back **LEONIDE MASSINE** (1895–1979) to replace Nijinsky. Massine was 19 and had little experience in ballet, but, under the guidance of Cecchetti, he soon became a remarkable dancer and mime and before long a choreographer of genius. When he married dancer Vera Savina, both had to leave the company and they toured with a group of their own, but Massine rejoined Diaghilev, 1925–1928. He later created ballets for the Paris companies of Etienne de Beaumont and Ida Rubinstein; Cochrane's Revue, London; the Roxy Theatre, N.Y.; Ballet Russe de Monte Carlo; Ballets des Champs-Elysées; Ballet Theatre, N.Y.; and others. Extraordinarily prolific, he became one of the greatest choreographers of the twentieth century, producing *Parade* (1917), *La Boutique Fantasque* and *Le Tricorne* (1919), *Pulcinella* (1920), *Le Beau Danube* (1924 and 1933) and the first symphonic ballets, *Choreartium* (Brahms, 1933), *La Symphonie Fantastique* (Berlioz, 1936),

98

Seventh Symphony (Beethoven, 1938), *Le Rouge et le Noir* (Shostakovitch, 1939). After Savina, he married dancers Eugenia Delarova and Tatiana Orlova and also Hannelore Holtwick. Author of *My Life in Ballet,* London, 1960. In Photo 97 he appears in *The Legend of Joseph* (Opéra, 1914), his first important role with the Ballets Russes. In Photo 98 he is seen in *Le Tricorne* (*The Three Cornered Hat,* London, 1919); having acquired great knowledge of Spanish dancing during a long stay with Diaghilev in Spain, Massine choreographed this masterpiece and danced the leading role. Photo 99 shows him with Tamara Toumanova in *La Symphonie Fantastique;* Photo 100, as the Peruvian in *Gaieté Parisienne,* 1938 revival; Photo 101, with Rosella Hightower (1920–) in *The New Yorker* (1940); Photo 102, in *Saratoga* (1941). (Photos 98–100: Gordon Anthony, London; Photos 101 & 102: Maurice Seymour, Chicago)

100

99

101

102

(Massine, *continued*)

103. VERA NEMTCHINOVA (1899–1984) in her most appealing role, in Nijinska's *Les Biches* (1924). People were shocked by the brevity of this costume, which Diaghilev himself had shortened; when Nemtchinova complained that she felt naked, he told her to put on gloves. She joined the Ballets Russes in 1915 and, after one brief defection, remained until 1926, creating a number of leading roles. With dancer Anatole Oboukhov (1895–1962), whom she married, and Anton Dolin she founded the Nemtchinova-Dolin Ballet, London, 1927–1928, and also appeared with the Ballets de Monte Carlo. She later taught for many years in New York. (Photo: Georges Detaille, Monte Carlo)

104

105

106

104–106. LEON WOIZIKOWSKI (1899–1975). A Polish dancer engaged by Diaghilev in 1916, he became famous in character roles and remained with the company until Diaghilev's death. Later he was in Pavlova's company, the Ballet Russe de Monte Carlo and the Ballet Russe of Colonel de Basil, taught in Warsaw at the opera school and was ballet master for the London Festival Ballet. His liaison with Sokolova lasted for many years but he finally returned to Poland in 1974 and died there. Photo 104 shows him in *Les Femmes de bonne humeur* (1917); Photo 105, as the Fox (below), in *Le Renard* (1922) with Nicholas Efimov (dates unknown; a dancer who fled Russia in 1921 with Balanchine and Danilova and then joined the Ballets Russes); Photo 106, in 1927. See also Photo 80. (Photo 106: Lenare, London)

107

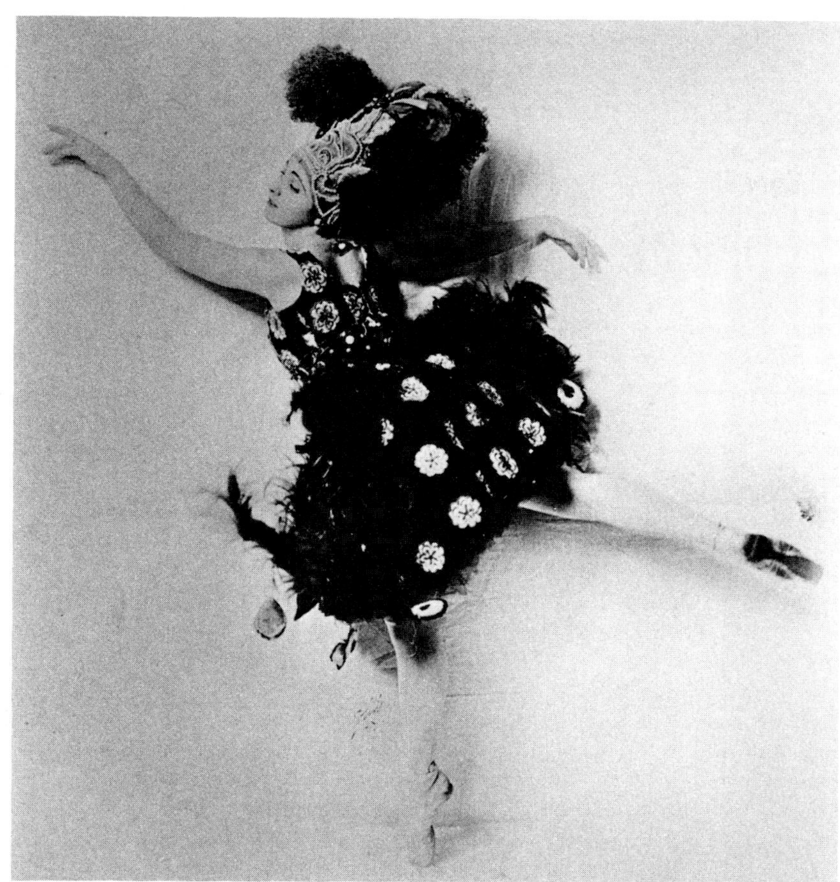

108

New stars of the Ballets Russes 1916–1917 American tours included the dancers in Photos 107–113. **107. XENIA MAKLEZOWA** (1893–1974) as the Firebird. A Moscow dancer with good technique, she was hired by Diaghilev to replace Karsavina. However, she made jealous scenes about publicity given to others and was so enraged by Lopokova's great popularity with the American public that she simply walked out. (Photo: White, N.Y., 1916) **108. NICHOLAS ZVEREV** (ca. 1897–1965) in *Le Pavillon d'Armide*. Although this dancer had been with Diaghilev for four years, he assumed a sudden new importance during the American tour. It was said that sometimes when Nijinsky's name was on the program, Zverev—supposedly a "look-alike"—substituted for him with no one the wiser. Zverev remained with the Ballets Russes until 1926 and then toured with his wife Nemtchinova (who later divorced him and married Oboukhov) and subsequently worked with the Brussels Théâtre de la Monnaie, at Boris Kniaseff's ballet school, Lausanne, and at the Teatro Colón, Buenos Aires. (Photo: White, N.Y.)

109

110

109 & 110. FLORE REVALLES (dates unknown). Opera singer and protégée of Metropolitan Opera director Otto Kahn, she was taken into the Ballets Russes to perform roles that did not require much technical training. In Photo 109 she is seen in *Schéhérazade;* in Photo 110, in *Cléopâtre.* (Photo 109: Count Jean de Strelecki, 1916; Photo 110: White, N.Y., 1916)

111–113. OLGA SPESSIVTSEVA (1895–). She was perhaps the only dancer contemporary with Pavlova who was considered the latter's equal. Cecchetti once said that an apple had been born and, when cut in two, one half was Pavlova and the other Spessivtseva. Diaghilev added that Spessivtseva was the half that had been turned to the sun. Although she danced with the Ballets Russes, 1916, it was in the U.S.A. and Diaghilev never saw her until she came to London for *The Sleeping Princess,* 1921. In between she returned to the Maryinsky but was with Diaghilev again, 1927–1928. From 1924 to 1932 she was much of the time at the Opéra. In 1943, while in New York, she suffered a mental breakdown which lasted until 1963, when she was well enough to be transferred from the State Institution to the Tolstoy Farm in suburban New York, where she now lives in retirement. Author of *Technique for the Ballet Artist,* London, 1967. In Photo 111 she is seen in *Esmeralda,* St. Petersburg. In Photo 112 she appears as Giselle, her greatest role; in Photo 113, in *La Chatte,* a role that she created in 1927 and was soon taken over by Diaghilev dancer Alice Nikitina. The photograph is autographed to Doubrovska from "Spessiva," the name she used in English-speaking countries. (Photo 113: G. I. Manuel, Paris)

111

112

113

114

115

116

114. LYDIA KYASHT (1885–1959) as the Firebird (1919). After appearing at the Maryinsky, Kyasht succeeded Adeline Genée at the Empire Theatre, London, 1908, joined Diaghilev in 1919 and later had her own company in London. Author of *Romantic Recollections,* London, 1929. **115. MARGARET CRASKE** (1892–). By the time Craske joined Diaghilev in 1920, he had a number of English dancers in the company. After a year she had to leave because of a foot injury, but she became assistant teacher to Maestro Cecchetti and then spent seven years in India absorbing the teachings of a guru. She has since taught for Sadler's Wells Ballet, Ballet Theatre, Metropolitan Opera School and Juilliard School and at present teaches at the Diana Byers School in New York. Co-author, with Cyril Beaumont, of *The Theory and Practice of Allegro in Classical Ballet,* London, 1946. **116.** While his company was performing in Madrid in early spring, 1921, Diaghilev, accompanied by Stravinsky and Boris Kochno, took a brief vacation in Seville, where he had the idea of staging a suite of flamenco dances for the coming London season. He engaged, among others, a beautiful Andalusian gipsy, Pepita Ramoje, renaming her **MARIA DALBAICIN** (dates unknown), and she had a resounding success in *Quadro Flamenco* (May 1921). Unlike the unfortunate Felix Fernández, brought to London to help with *Le Tricorne,* but so unable to adjust either to London or the Ballets Russes that he went mad and spent the rest of his life in an English insane asylum, Dalbaicin adapted immediately to her new surroundings. She stayed on to appear in the leading role of *Le Tricorne* and in *The Sleeping Princess* (November 1921) and before long was even a frequenter of Paris nightclubs. (Photo: Mme. S. Georges, London)

117

118

Another galaxy was added for the spectacular production of Diaghilev's *The Sleeping Princess,* November 2, 1921. Lubov Egorova, Vera Trefilova and Olga Spessivtseva alternated as Princess Aurora, occasionally replaced by Lopokova and Nemtchinova. Ludmila Schollar returned to the company, this time with a husband, Anatole Vilzak; Pierre Vladimirov came back bringing a wife, Felia Doubrovska. Anton Dolin, age 17, made a first appearance in the corps. **117 & 118. VERA TREFILOVA** (1875–1943). A sparkling prima ballerina at the Maryinsky after 1906, dashing off 32 fouettés with ease, she shone especially as Princess Aurora, but resigned in 1910 because of Kchessinska's jealous intrigues. In 1917 she opened a school in Paris. Photo 117 shows her as a youngster in St. Petersburg; Photo 118, as Princess Aurora in *The Sleeping Princess,* London, 1921. Diaghilev ignored the telegram Trefilova sent the night before the premiere, reminding him of her age (46) and threatening suicide if he did not release her from her contact. However, she had a dazzling success, continued with Diaghilev in Paris and Monte Carlo, 1923, and then retired.

119. LUBOV EGOROVA (1880–1972) at the Maryinsky in a revival of Petipa's *The Blue Dahlia.* Egorova graduated in 1898 and was promoted ballerina at the Maryinsky, 1912. After appearing with Diaghilev, she opened a school in Paris, 1923, and founded Le Ballet de la Jeunesse, 1937. Her adored and adoring husband, Prince Nikita Troubetskoy, bought a house in the Paris suburbs for her retirement, but it was lost through mismanagement after he and their son died, and Egorova ended her days alone in a home for the aged and indigent. A delightful performer but even greater teacher, she numbered among her students Ethery Pagava, Muriel Belmondo (sister of Jean-Paul and great-granddaughter of Cerrito) and even Scott Fitzgerald's wife Zelda. (Photo: K. A. Fisher, St. Petersburg)

120

121

120. PIERRE VLADIMIROV (1893–1970) in *Les Sylphides,* 1928, with Pavlova, with whom he toured, 1928–1931. Apart from early Ballets Russes seasons, 1912–1914, Vladimirov was at the Maryinsky until 1918, danced Prince Charming in Diaghilev's *The Sleeping Princess,* then toured with Karsavina, the Mordkin Ballet and Pavlova, settled in New York and taught at the School of American Ballet. (Photo: Ross, Berlin) **121. ANATOLE VILZAK** (1898–) in Fokine's *Don Juan* (1936). He was premier danseur at the Maryinsky, 1917. In 1921, he joined Diaghilev, then Ida Rubinstein's company and the Ballet Russe de Monte Carlo. With his wife Ludmila Schollar, he opened the Vilzak-Schollar School in New York, 1940, was a frequent guest teacher elsewhere and settled in California on the staff of the San Francisco ballet school.

122

123

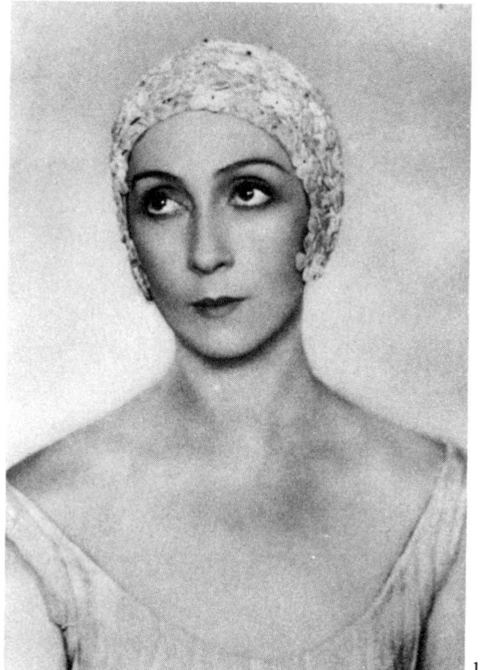

124

122–125. **FELIA DOUBROVSKA** (1896–1981). Accepted at the Maryinsky in 1913, Doubrovska joined Diaghilev, 1921, and created the Bride in *Les Noces* (1923), a Muse in *Apollon Musagète* (1928) and the Siren in *The Prodigal Son* (1929), after which the company disbanded. She then danced in Buenos Aires and at the Metropolitan Opera and was a distinguished teacher at the American School of Ballet until the age of 84. Photo 122 shows her as the Firebird; Photo 123, as the Hostess in *Les Biches* (1924). When she took over this role from Nijinska, she complained to Diaghilev that she was too tall for the costume. "You have perfect taste," he told her; "go to Chanel and order anything you like." In Photo 124 she is seen in *Apollon Musagète* (1928); in Photo 125, in *Ode,* looking like a modern New York City Ballet dancer in the costume by Pavel Tchelichev, which seemed too modern and quite scandalous in 1928. See also Photo 138. (Photo 122: Lipnitzki, Paris; Photo 123: Raphael, London; Photo 125: Madame Yevonde)

125

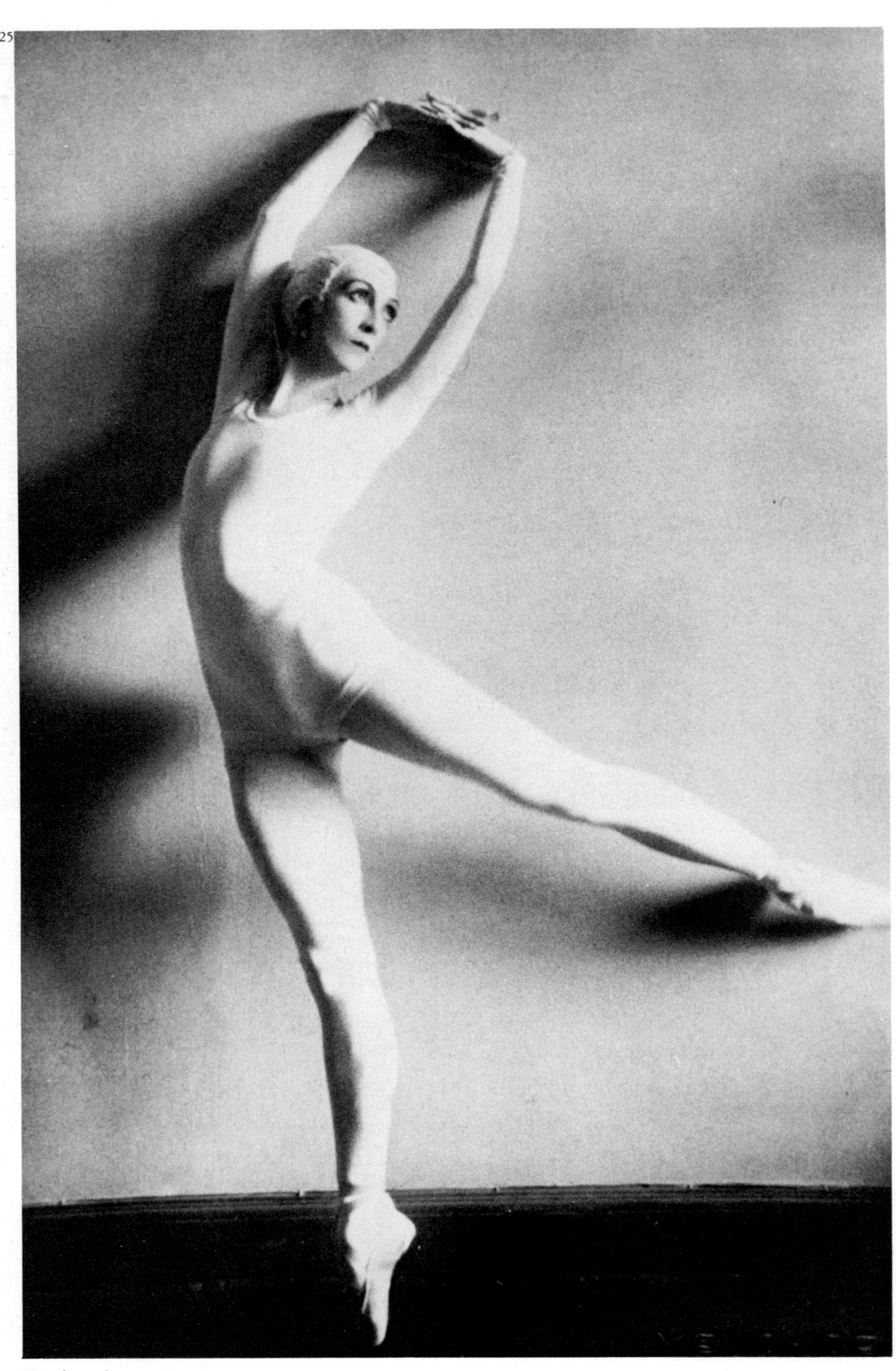

(Doubrovska, *continued*)

126. ALICE NIKITINA (1909–1978) in *Barabau* (1925). After studying at St. Petersburg's Imperial Ballet School, Nikitina appeared in Vienna, with Boris Romanoff's company in Berlin and with the Ballets Russes, 1923–1929, where the munificent donations to the company by her two protectors, Lord Rothermere and Vincent Bendix, did much to further her career and obtain leading roles for her. Elegant, slim and vain, she nevertheless graciously accepted comic roles as in *Barabau.* Later she danced with various companies and, in 1938, embarked on a new life as coloratura soprano in Italy. She finally had her own school in Paris, astonishing everyone by teaching in black leotards with all her Rothermere-Bendix jewels. Author of *Nikitina by Herself,* London, 1959. See also Photo 133. (Photo: Beck & MacGregor)
127 & 128. MICHEL PAVLOFF (Michel Liberson, 1891–1981). As he began his ballet career too late, he had only minor roles with the Ballets Russes, but was a very useful and popular company member. In the Monte Carlo revival of *Les Femmes de bonne humeur,* he took over Madame Cecchetti's role (Photo 127) and reported that Picasso himself had equipped him with a "bosom," painting it on before performances. Later he ran a Paris nightclub and managed the Ice Capades' European tour. Photo 128 shows him at age 85 in front of Léon Bakst's design for his costume. See also Photo 139. (Photo 128: Louis Péres)

127

126

128

129

130

131

129–131. **SERGE LIFAR** (1905–). Imported by Nijinska from Kiev, where he had studied at her school, Lifar joined the Ballets Russes in 1923. Inept at the beginning, he soon had the leading roles in *Apollon Musagète* and *The Prodigal Son* as his greatest achievements. After Diaghilev's death, he danced at the Paris Opéra and choreographed some 20 ballets. Accused of being a Nazi collaborator during World War II, he left for Monte Carlo, 1945, danced there and choreographed another series of ballets. At the Paris Opéra again, 1947–1958, he produced another half-dozen ballets and became opinionated and despotic. Organizer of ballet art exhibitions and author of some 25 books, historical biographies, technique manuals and a life of Diaghilev. Photo 129 shows him in *Apollon Musagète* (1928); Photo 130, in *Barabau* (1925); Photo 131, in *The Prodigal Son* (1929). See also Photos 133 and 138. (Photo 129: Lipnitzki, Paris; Photo 130: Man Ray)

132

132 & 133. TAMARA GEVA (Tamara Gevergeyeva, 1908–   ) left Russia with her husband Georgi Balanchivadze (Balanchine), Alexandra Danilova and Nicholas Efimov. They appeared in the West in 1924 as Soviet State dancers and all four were engaged by Diaghilev. Geva appeared in minor roles in *La Pastorale, The Triumph of Neptune* and other ballets. She came with the Chauve-Souris to the U.S.A., where she had a brilliant career in stage musicals, including *Whoopee* and *On Your Toes,* and in films. Directed a BBC Television documentary on Diaghilev, 1981, and published her autobiography, *Split Seconds,* New York, 1972. In Photo 133 she is at the far left; the others are Lubov Tchernicheva, Alice Nikitina, Alexandra Danilova and Serge Lifar, all in *La Pastorale* (1926). (Photo 132: Alfred Cheney Johnston; Photo 133: *Daily Sketch,* London)

133

134

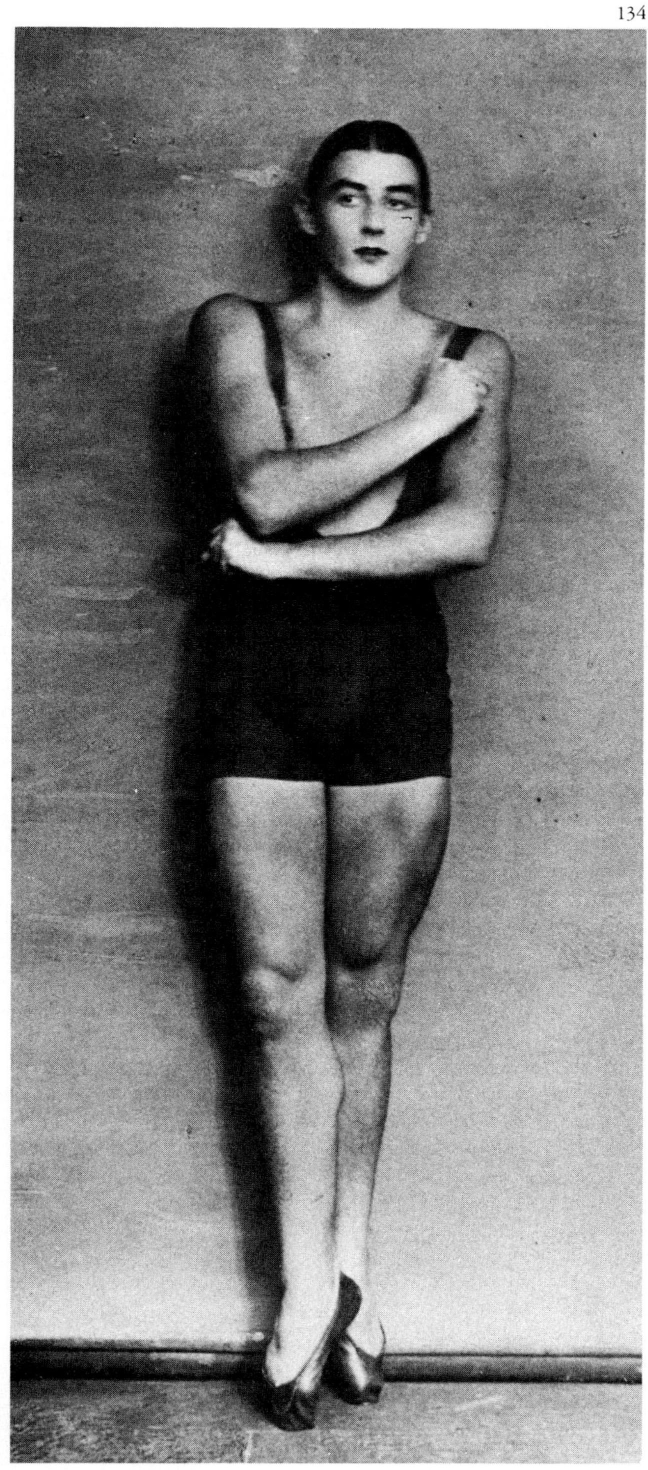

135

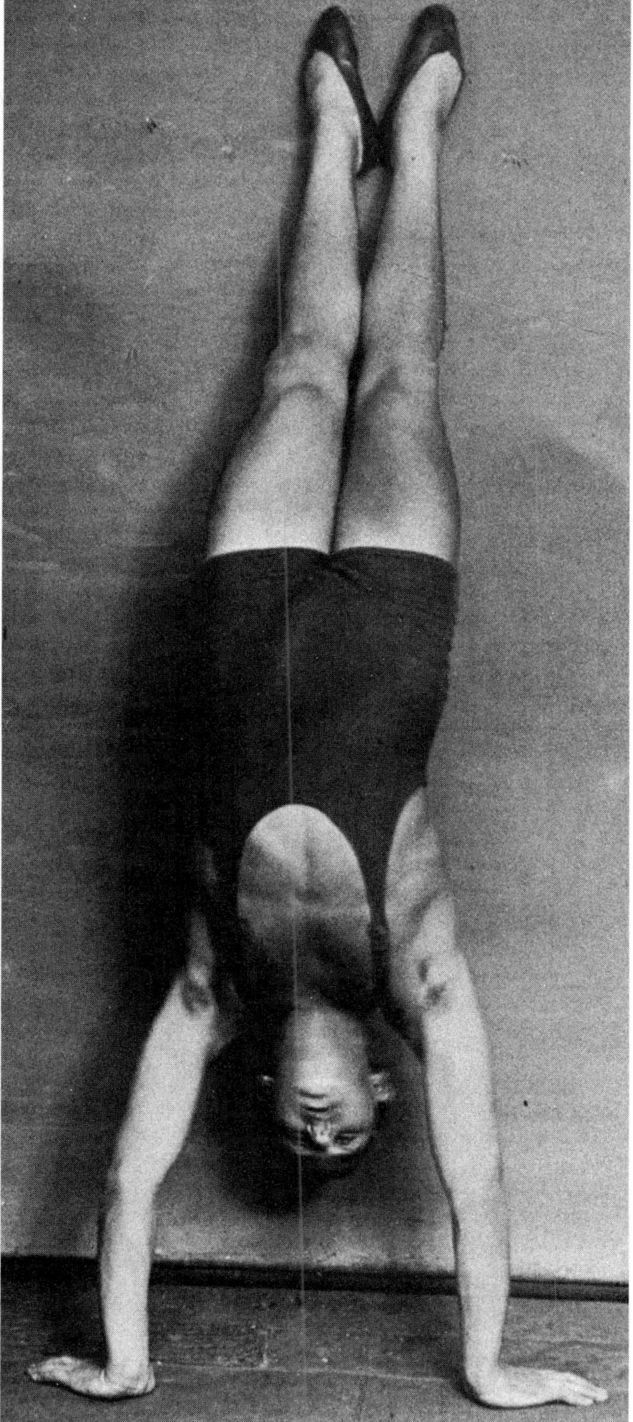

134–138. ANTON DOLIN (Patrick Healey-Kay, 1904–1983). In Photos 134 and 135 he is practicing for Nijinska's flippant ballet *Le Train Bleu* (1924). Dolin had left Diaghilev after *The Sleeping Princess,* but returned as soloist in 1924; seeing his antics in *Le Train Bleu,* few could have imagined the great classical dancer he would become. After Diaghilev's death his most important venture was as founder-director-soloist of the Markova-Dolin Ballet, 1935–1938 and 1945–1948. In between, he appeared with Ballet Theatre, New York, and did much to promote the best aspects of classic ballet while also being delightfully comic, as in *Bluebeard* (1941).

136

(Dolin, *continued*). He appeared with many companies and from 1927 was an able choreographer of his own new works and of conscientious restorations, such as his celebrated version of Perrot's *Pas de Quatre*. Author of many books, including biographies of Markova and Spessivtseva. In his eightieth year he was still busy with teaching, reviving ballets and public speaking. Photo 136 shows him as L'Elégant in *Les Fâcheux* (1924); Photo 137, in 1981. Photo 138 shows him with Felia Doubrovska and Serge Lifar in *Le Bal* (1929), produced by the Ballets Russes only three months before Diaghilev's death (music by Vittorio Rieti, decor and costumes by Giorgio de Chirico, choreography by Balanchine). See also Photo 139. (Photo 136: Georges Detaille, Monte Carlo; Photo 138: Lipnitzki, Paris)

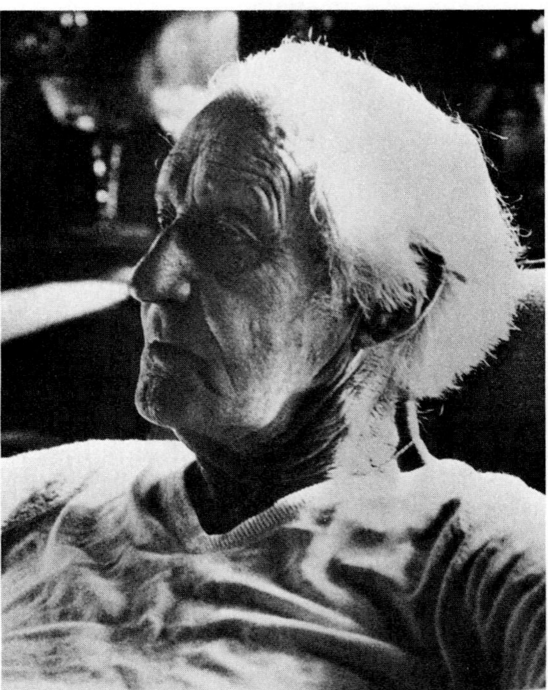

137

138

139

140

141

139–142. ALICIA MARKOVA (Lilian Alicia Marks, 1910–   ). When Markova was engaged by Diaghilev she was only 15, but within a year she had the title role in *Le Rossignol* (1925) and then many ballerina roles until 1929. Afterwards she danced in the Markova-Dolin Ballet, with Ballet Rambert and with Vic-Wells Ballet, creating important roles in Frederick Ashton creations; and appeared with Ballet Russe de Monte Carlo, where she was sensational in *Le Rouge et le Noir* (1939). With Ballet Theatre she shone in the great classic roles and Antony Tudor's *Romeo and Juliet* (1943), and she continued as guest ballerina with many companies until she retired, 1962. Tiny, ethereal, but with an incisive technique, she is considered one of the twentieth century's greatest dancers. Author of *Giselle and I,* London, 1960. Photo 139 shows her in Monte Carlo, 1926, with Anton Dolin and Michel Pavloff. Photo 140 shows her in *La Chatte,* at age 17; she took over this role from Spessivtseva and Nikitina. In Photo 141 she is seen in *Giselle,* which she often performed with Anton Dolin. They became romantically famous as partners, as Karsavina/Nijinsky had been, and later Danilova/Franklin, Fonteyn/Nureyev and Fracci/Bruhn were to be.

142

In Photo 142 she is seen in *Romeo and Juliet* (1943) with Hugh Laing (see Photo 225) as Romeo and Dimitri Romanoff as Friar Lawrence. **DIMITRI ROMANOFF** (1907–) danced on tour with Nini Theilade and with San Francisco Ballet before joining Ballet Theatre, where he became régisseur, 1946. At present he is teaching in California. For Markova, see also Photo 179. (Photo 141: Annemarie Heinrich, Buenos Aires)

144

143

143–147. ALEXANDRA DANILOVA (1904–   ) came to the West as a member of the Soviet State Ballet (GATOB) with Tamara Geva, Balanchine and Efimov and was engaged by Diaghilev, for whom she danced leading roles until 1929. With Colonel de Basil, 1933–1938, and Ballet Russe de Monte Carlo, 1938–1952, she created many roles for Massine and Balanchine and shone in all the classic ballets, her sparkle in *Gaieté Parisienne* (revival) and *Le Beau Danube* (1933 version) being especially admired. She was adored by the public for her elegance, charm and vivacity, and the audience wept at the gala when she retired. She now teaches at the American School of Ballet, and travels in Europe and the U.S.A., coaching and restaging ballets. She appeared in the film *The Turning Point* (1977) and in Anne Belle's documentary *Reflections of a Dancer* (1981). Photo 143 shows her as Pulcinella for Diaghilev's Ballets Russes; Photo 144, as the Firebird, Ballet Russe de Monte Carlo, 1941; Photo 145, as the Sugar Plum Fairy, Ballet Russe de Monte Carlo; Photo 146, as Odette in *Swan Lake;* Photo 147 at Diaghilev's grave, Island of San Michele, Venice. See also Photo 133. (Photo 147: Niki Ekstrom, N.Y., 1979)

145

146

147

(Danilova, *continued*)

148

148 & 149. GEORGE BALANCHINE (Georgi Balanchivadze, 1904–1983). One of the greatest and most prolific choreographers in ballet history, rivaled only by Jules Perrot and Marius Petipa. Balanchine graduated, 1921, then joined the Soviet State Ballet, while also training as a musician. During a tour in the West with Soviet dancers, he was engaged by Diaghilev. Already known in Russia for his controversial ballets, he became Diaghilev's chief and last choreographer, producing, among others, two enduring masterpieces, *Apollon Musagète* (1928) and *The Prodigal Son* (1929). After working with the Royal Danish Ballet, Ballet Russe de Monte Carlo and his own Ballets 1933, he was brought to the U.S.A. by Lincoln Kirstein, 1934, and they established the American School of Ballet and American Ballet Company. Balanchine's next major venture, Ballet Society, 1946, became, in 1948, the New York City Ballet, of which he was director until his death. His hundreds of creations include not only achievements such as *Serenade* (1934), *Concerto Barocco* (1940) and *Agon* (1957), but also revivals, with Danilova, of *Raymonda* and *Coppélia*, new versions of *The Firebird* and *Pulcinella*, operas, musical comedies, films and television. His collaboration with Stravinsky, begun when he was 21, culminated in three festivals, at the Metropolitan Opera, 1947, and at Lincoln Center, 1972 and 1982. He married ballerinas Tamara Geva, Vera Zorina, Maria Tallchief and Tanaquil Le Clercq. Photo 148 shows him in Venice, on holiday with Diaghilev, 1925; Photo 149 shows him in 1981 during preparations for his television version of *L'Enfant et les Sortilèges* (first produced in Monte Carlo, 1925). (Photo 149: Don Perdue)

149

MID-TWENTIETH CENTURY

150

151

150 & 151. RUTH PAGE (1905–). Leading native-born American ballerina and choreographer of astonishing productivity; it would hardly be an exaggeration to say that Ruth Page danced or choreographed for almost everyone. She was not with the Ballets Russes long enough to be considered a Diaghilev ballerina, but she toured with Pavlova, 1918, and with Adolph Bolm, for whom she created Terpsichore in his pre-Diaghilev *Apollon Musagète* (Washington, D.C., 1928); appeared, 1933, with an all-black company and with Harald Kreutzberg, 1932–1934, with the Chicago and Metropolitan Operas, and with revues, traveling all over Europe, Russia, Japan, North and South America. Mainly she has been the guiding spirit of ballet in Chicago. She has made a specialty of adapting operas and operettas for ballet and using American as well as classic subjects, and is continuing to produce new works. First married to the late Thomas H. Fisher, in 1983 she married the French artist André Delfau, who has designed many ballets for her. Author of *Page by Page,* New York, 1978. Photo 150 shows her in classic tutu, in what her teacher Cecchetti described as a perfect arabesque. Photo 151 shows her in the "sack" designed for her by sculptor Isamu Noguchi for *Expanding Universe* (1932). Page has always worked with the leading and most avant-garde artists and composers.

152

152. HUBERT STOWITTS (1892–1953) in an Indo-Chinese dance. While he was a student at a California university, Pavlova engaged this extraordinary young athlete, who had no professional ballet training, but soon became her partner and then designed and staged ballets for her. After leaving her, he appeared in France and England, studied dance in the Orient and then devoted the rest of his life to painting, with exhibitions in leading European and American galleries. A first biography of this many-faceted personality, by Lynn Garafola, is in preparation. See also Photo 63. (Photo: E. O. Hoppé)

153

154

Two American dancers who vigorously promoted ballet in the U.S.A. **153. LEW CHRISTENSEN** (1909–1984), like his brothers William (1902–) and Harold (1904–), studied with his uncle Peter Christensen in Salt Lake City. He joined American Ballet and taught at the school, became ballet master, New York City Ballet, and then director-choreographer of the San Francisco Ballet, a position he occupied with immense success. (Photo: Maurice Seymour, Chicago) **154. GISELLA CACCIALANZA** (1914–), wife of Lew Christensen, studied with Cecchetti (about whom she wrote "Letters from the Maestro," *Dance Perspectives,* 1945), danced with Ballet Caravan and Ballet Society, creating leading roles for Balanchine, and now resides in San Francisco. (Photo: Maurice Seymour, Chicago)

155. SERGE OUKRAINSKY (Leonides Orlay de Carva, 1885–1972). Son of wealthy Russian aristocrats, he grew up in Paris and did not begin to study until he was 25. Three years later (1913), he was engaged by Pavlova and traveled with her all over the U.S.A., back to Europe and Russia and again to Chicago. During that two-year tour he met Pavley, with whom he set up a school in Chicago and then the Pavley-Oukrainsky Ballet, a company for which they choreographed all the ballets and which functioned, with few interruptions, until Pavley's death, 1931. Oukrainsky settled in California in 1934, taught for a while, outlived Pavley by 41 years and died in poverty. **156. ANDREAS PAVLEY** (Andreas van Dorph deWeyer, 1892–1931). Dutch dancer who studied at The Hague and in Paris with Ivan Clustine (1862–1941, a Bolshoi dancer who had a school and then was ballet master, 1909–1914, at the Opéra) and Emile Jaques-Dalcroze. By age 17 Pavley had staged a ballet spectacular in Amsterdam. With Oukrainsky, he made the long tour with Pavlova and was dancer-choreographer of the Pavley-Oukrainsky Ballet, which he took on tour to Mexico and Latin America.

155

156

157

157. NINETTE DE VALOIS (Edris Stannus, 1890–), Irish dancer, choreographer, teacher. She and Marie Rambert were the two pioneers in establishing British ballet, their efforts resulting in a national company and unexcelled performers and choreographers. Dame Ninette, after short stints with revues, Diaghilev's Ballets Russes and other companies, founded a school in London that produced the Vic-Wells Ballet, which then became Sadler's Wells Ballet and finally, in 1956, the Royal Ballet, established at Covent Garden. She choreographed many successful ballets, is the author of *Invitation to the Ballet* (1937) and is the recipient of many decorations and awards. (Photo: Gerard Murrell, N.Y., 1981) **158. FREDERICK ASHTON** (1904–) in *Nocturne,* 1936. One of the most important twentieth-century choreographers, he danced with Ballet Rambert and Ida Rubinstein's company, joined the Vic-Wells as choreographer, 1935, and was director of the Royal Ballet, 1963–1970. Sir Frederick has produced a series of masterworks for British and foreign companies which are constantly revived, favorites being *Les Patineurs* (1937), *Scènes de ballet* and *Cinderella* (1948), *Illuminations* (1950) and a ravishing re-creation of *La Fille mal gardée* (1960). Recipient of many decorations and awards, British, French, Danish and American. **159. SALLY GILMOUR** (1921–). Leading dancer of the Ballet Rambert, she created many important roles and retired in 1953. (Photo: J. W. Debenham, London)

158

159

160

160. MAUD LLOYD (1908–) in Ashton's *The Passionate Pavane.* One of the first ballerinas of Ballet Rambert, 1927–1938, then co-director of Antony Tudor's London Ballet, she created many roles for both Tudor and Ashton. Co-author with her husband, Nigel Gosling (pseudonym Alexander Bland), of ballet criticism for magazines and newspapers, books about Elie Nadelman, Margot Fonteyn and Nureyev, and *A History of Dance and Ballet* (1976). **161 & 162. ANYA LINDEN** (Anna Eltenton, 1933–) joined Sadler's Wells Ballet in 1951, was promoted ballerina in 1958 and created roles in ballets by Ashton and John Cranko. Retired in 1965. Photo 161 shows her in *Prince of the Pagodas* (1957); Photo 162, as Cinderella. (Photo 161: Antony Armstrong-Jones; Photo 162: Roy Round) **163. SVETLANA BERIOSOVA** (1932–) in the *Raymonda* pas de deux. She studied at the Vilzak-Schollar School, New York, and in 1947 joined the Ballet Russe de Monte Carlo, where her father Nicholas Beriosov (1906–) was also dancing. By 1955, she was ballerina of Sadler's Wells and then one of the greatest attractions of the Royal Ballet as well as an important guest star until she retired, 1975. (Photo: Dominic, London)

161

162

163

164. JOHN GILPIN (1930–1983). After starting his career as a child actor, Gilpin joined Ballet Rambert, 1945, and soon was promoted premier danseur. He was appointed director of London Festival Ballet, 1962–1965. Acclaimed as a brilliant performer, he had, with frequent interruptions due to surgical operations, performed with many companies in England, France and Japan. First married to Sally Judd, he was married two months before he died to Princess Antoinette of Monaco. **165. MERLE PARK** (1937–) as the Firebird. A native of Rhodesia, by age 22 she was première danseuse of Sadler's Wells Ballet. Now a star of the Royal Ballet, she is a charming interpreter of both classic and contemporary roles and, as of 1983, is Director of the Royal School of Ballet. (Photo: Roy Round)

165

164

166–170. Dame **MARGOT FONTEYN** (Peggy Hookham, 1919–). Most celebrated British ballerina of the twentieth century, she made her debut, 1934, with the Vic-Wells Ballet and then became première danseuse with Sadler's Wells and the Royal Ballet, especially known as creator of roles in works by Ashton as well as all the classics. When Rudolph Nureyev (1938–), first major defector from Russia's Kirov, was established as semipermanent guest artist at the Royal Ballet during the 1960s, he became Dame Margot Fonteyn's constant partner and she was launched on a second phase of her career. Recipient of many awards and decorations, she was appointed President of the Royal Academy of Dancing, 1954, and Chancellor of Durham University, 1982, and is the author of *Margot Fonteyn: Autobiography,* New York, 1976, and *The Magic of Dance,* New York, 1979, which also appeared as a BBC television series. In Photo 166 she is seen at age 14; in Photos 167 and 168, she is with Nureyev in *Marguerite and Armand* (1963).

167

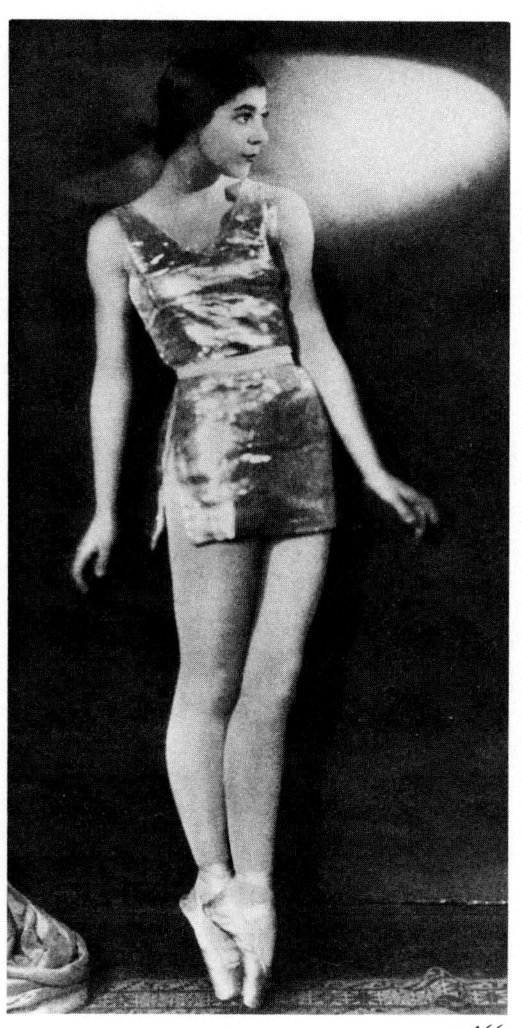

166

168

169

170

(Fonteyn, *continued*). In Photo 169, she is seen as the Firebird; in Photo 170, in her robes of office as Chancellor of Durham University. (Photo 166: E. O. Hoppé; Photo 167: Cecil Beaton; Photo 168: Dominic, London; Photo 169: Houston Roger, London)

171

172

171 & 172. CLÉO DE MÉRODE (Cléopâtre-Diane de Mérode, 1881–1966). There is a tendency to classify Cléo de Mérode with "les grandes horizontales" of the Belle Epoque, as she was extraordinarily beautiful and accumulated a multitude of much-publicized admirers—the Maharajah of Karpurthala wanted to marry her and King Léopold of Belgium was so attentive that the press nicknamed him "Cléopold." Nevertheless, the ravishing Cléo was a serious ballerina who entered the Paris Opéra school at the age of eight, graduated and appeared in solo roles. During the Paris Exposition of 1900, much impressed with the dances and costumes of the Far East, she explored their possibilities and became one of the earliest performers to appear in well-researched oriental dance. Her brilliant career took her all over Europe and the U.S.A. and she was still astonishingly beautiful at the age of 85. Author of *Le Ballet de Ma Vie,* Paris, 1955. Photo 171 shows her at the Paris Opéra, ca. 1900. Photo 172 shows the hair style to which she adhered all her life and which created a fashion in Paris. **173. YVETTE CHAUVIRÉ** (1917–) in a pose from *Swan Lake.* French ballet at the Paris Opéra was at a low ebb during the time of Cléo de Mérode, with only foreign stars Rosita Mauri and Carlotta Zambelli upholding the former high standards. However, during the 1930s, brilliant native French dancers emerged, such as Lycette Darsonval (1912–) and Chauviré. The latter became première danseuse étoile in 1941, and remained the leading attraction at the Opéra for 30 years, while also maintaining an international reputation as a scintillating technician in new as well as classical roles. Author of *Je suis ballerine,* Paris, 1960.

173

174. **MICHEL RENAULT** (1927–). After graduating from the Paris Opéra school, Renault was promoted to the rank of premier danseur étoile at the age of 19, the youngest dancer ever to have achieved that rank in the history of the Opéra. For 13 years he continued as a spectacular performer both in Paris and abroad and then retired to devote himself to choreography and teaching. (Photo: Serge Lido)

175

175. **ETHERY PAGAVA** (1931–) in costume for *La Somnambule.* A pupil of Egorova, she appeared when only 14 with the Ballets des Champs-Elysées in *Les Forains* (1945), capturing the public with her ethereal, elusive charm. She later performed with the Marquis de Cuevas Ballet, the company of Janine Charrat and in Holland and at Italy's International Festival, Nervi. (Photo: Serge Lido)

176

177

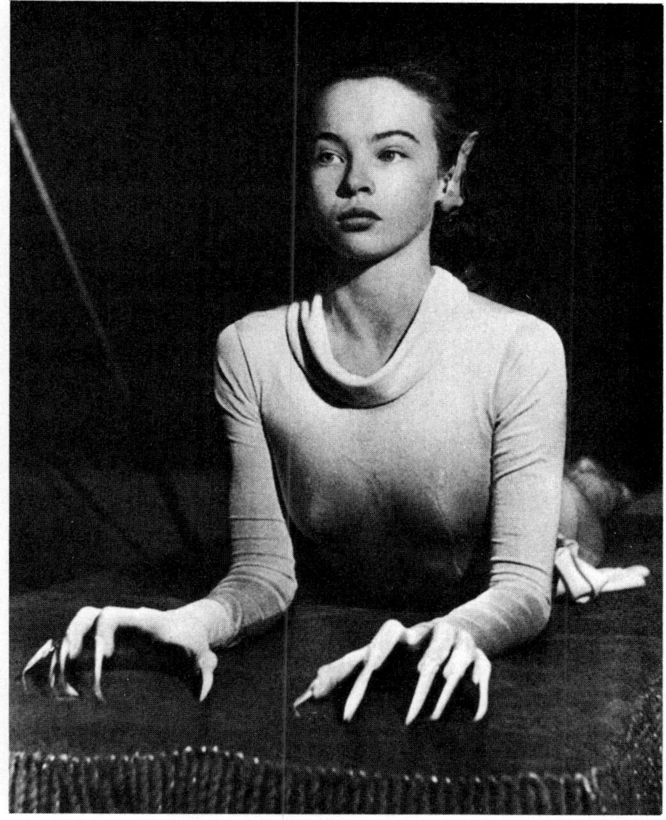

176. JEAN BABILÉE (Jean Gutman, 1923–   ) in *Le Portrait de Don Quixote* (1947). In addition to his splendid technique acquired from studies at the Paris Opéra with Kniaseff, Volinine and Gsovsky, Babilée had a rare expressiveness of face and gesture which made him a unique interpreter and performer. He was the danseur étoile of the Ballet des Champs-Elysées and the Ballets de Paris, 1945 and 1947, and made a deep impression in *Le Jeune Homme et la Mort* (1946) and *La Rencontre, ou Oedipe et le Sphinx* (1948). He has appeared at La Scala, with Ballet Theatre, at the Metropolitan and Paris Operas and at festivals in Italy, Brazil, Israel and Edinburgh, besides touring with his own company, 1956. Married to Nathalie Philippart, who shared his appearances with Les Ballets des Champs-Elysées. (Photo: Serge Lido)

177. LESLIE CARON (1931–   ) in *La Rencontre, ou Oedipe et le Sphinx* (1948). Her debut coincided with her appearance in the leading role of *La Rencontre* for Les Ballets des Champs-Elysées. In 1951, she appeared in Gene Kelly's film *An American in Paris,* performed for Roland Petit's Ballets de Paris, 1954, and has been busy as a cinema actress, starring in *Lili* (1953), *Daddy Long Legs* (1955), *Gigi* (1958), *Fanny* (1961) and many other films. (Photo: Serge Lido)

178

179

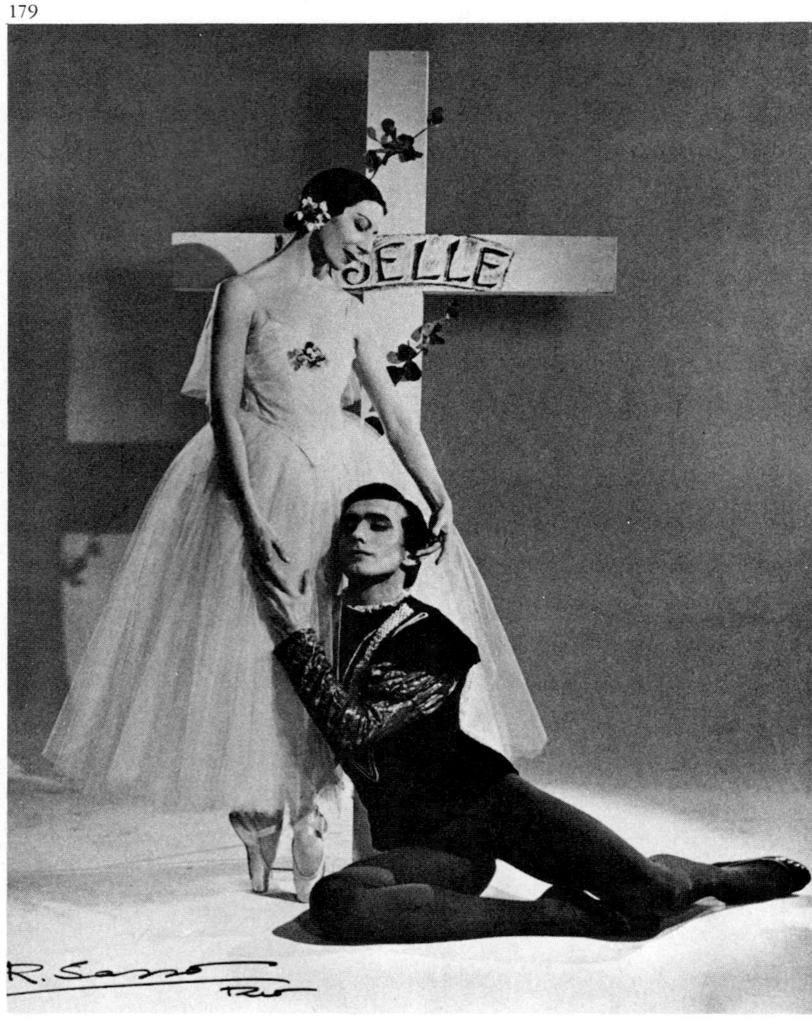

178 & 179. OLEG BRIANSKY (1929–). Belgian-born dancer, choreographer, teacher. He formed his own small company in Brussels when he was only 16. He was successively with Les Ballets des Champs-Elysées, Ballets de Paris, London Festival Ballet, Chicago Opera Ballet and others and considered an Adonis and a great stylist as danseur noble. His performances were brought to a halt by a back injury, but his active career continues as a much sought-after choreographer and reviver of ballets in North and South America and Europe. He directs and teaches at his New York school with his wife Mireille Briane as partner and also directs the school at the Saratoga, New York, Ballet Center. In Photo 178 he is seen in *Swan Lake,* Paris, 1951; in Photo 179, with Alicia Markova in *Giselle.* (Photo 179: R. Sasso, Rio de Janeiro)

180. MILORAD MISKOVITCH (1928–). Born in Yugoslavia, he has appeared with companies all over the world, but Miskovitch remains very much a personality of the Parisian scene, where he studied with Kniaseff and Preobrajenska and first appeared with the Ballets des Champs-Elysées. Since then he has performed with the company of Colonel de Basil, Ballets de Paris, Janine Charrat Company, Chicago Opera Ballet and many others in Europe and the Americas. A danseur noble of unusual elegance, he has been the partner of such celebrated ballerinas as Alicia Markova, Yvette Chauviré and Carla Fracci, as well as a choreographer and teacher. With Irene Lidova, author and wife of the photographer Serge Lido, he also founded a company of his own.

180

181

181–183. GALINA ULANOVA (1910–). After many of the foremost Russian dancers had departed for the West, either with Diaghilev or independently, new generations of brilliant Soviet performers emerged in Petrograd (Leningrad) and Moscow. Most admired and loved and also best known abroad was Ulanova. During her 34-year career, she appeared with both the Kirov and Bolshoi, was seen in Vienna, Rome, Florence, Venice, London and New York, and made films, especially *Romeo and Juliet* (1954), that reached a world-wide audience. Author of an autobiography and a book about her favorite ballets, she now teaches in Moscow. Photo 181 shows her with Mikhail Gabovich (1905–1965) in *Romeo and Juliet,* Moscow, 1946; Photo 182, as Cinderella, Bolshoi, 1945; Photo 183, as Giselle, Bolshoi, 1956.

182

184

184. MARINA SEMIONOVA (1908–   ) as Giselle at the Paris Opéra, 1935. Most resplendent of all the pupils of the celebrated Soviet teacher Agrippina Vaganova (1879–1951), Semionova was promoted ballerina of GATOB, 1926, and then prima ballerina at the Bolshoi, 1930–1952. She was guest artist at the Opéra, 1935–1936, in *Giselle,* with Serge Lifar as partner, and in excerpts from *Swan Lake* and *Divertissement.* Parisians, dazzled by her technique, found her insensitive as Giselle. After retiring, she remained at the Bolshoi as a teacher. (Photo: Viollet, Paris)

185

186

185. MAYA PLISETSKAYA (1925–). Having graduated from Moscow's Bolshoi ballet school, 1943, she joined the Bolshoi Ballet as a soloist and was promoted ballerina two years later. Her dazzling technique and dramatic power brought her all the leading roles in the classics, many revivals and Soviet ballets. She made a great impression in Fokine's *The Dying Swan* and has appeared extensively in films and on television. Her father, an engineer with a Soviet coal project in Spitzbergen, was removed by the authorities in 1937 and never heard from again, and her mother and an infant brother were sent to a labor camp. Maya and another brother were brought up by their maternal uncle, Asaf Messerer (1903–), Bolshoi dancer, ballet master and teacher, and his sister, Sulamith, also a dancer. Plisetskaya is married to the composer Rodion Shchedrin. Although tragedy haunted her childhood, today she is one of the greatest and most glamorous international ballerinas, having performed with Roland Petit and Maurice Béjart in Paris and in the U.S.A., Italy, Japan, New Zealand and East Berlin. She has choreographed several ballets and is the recipient of many awards. (Photo: Alise Ziverts, N.Y.) **186. IRINA KOLPAKOVA** (1933–) as Princess Aurora in *The Sleeping Beauty,* during a Kirov tour in the U.S.A. A Soviet dancer of incomparable grace and charm, Kolpakova joined the Kirov, 1951, created many roles and shone in the classics, especially *Giselle, Raymonda* and *The Sleeping Beauty.* Married Vladilen Semionov (1932–), who was always her partner until he retired, 1971. (Photo: Alise Ziverts, N.Y.)

187

187. YURI GRIGOROVICH (1927–) joined the Kirov, 1946, and became ballet master there, 1962. His first major choreographic work, *The Stone Flower,* was acclaimed at the Kirov, 1957, and is often performed in Russia and abroad. In 1964, Grigorovich was named Artistic Director of the Bolshoi and that company's official choreographer. Arriving in Moscow with his store of experiences from the Kirov and with his particular inclination toward the classics, he did much to soften the rather acrobatic image of the Bolshoi. Productions he staged included *The Sleeping Beauty, The Nutcracker, Swan Lake* and original works of his own, in many of which his wife, Natalia Bessmertnova, has had leading roles. (Photo: Nina Alovert, 1973)

188

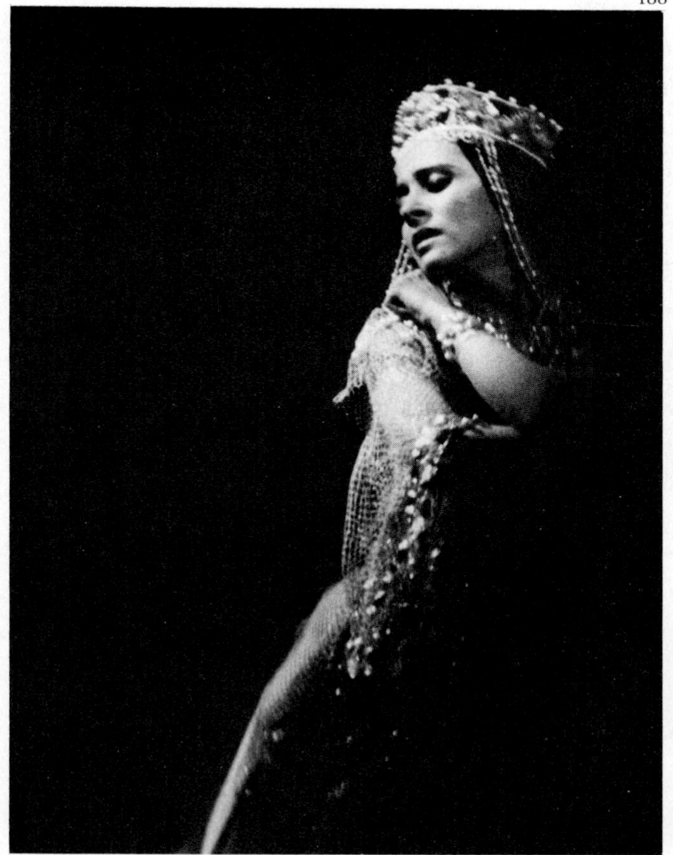

188 & 189. NATALIA BESSMERTNOVA (1941–). Born in Moscow, Bessmertnova studied at the Bolshoi school and joined the company in 1961. This dancer has a special appeal in lyrical, classical roles but has also starred in ballets by her husband Yuri Grigorovich. She has received awards in Varna and Paris. Photo 188 shows her in *Ivan the Terrible;* Photo 189, with Mikhail Baryshnikov in rehearsal for *Giselle,* Kirov, 1974. (Photos: Nina Alovert)

189

190

190 & 191. ERIK BRUHN (1928–). After the period of Hans Beck, the Royal Danish Ballet suffered a decline, but during the 1930s and 1940s, with Harald Lander (1905–1971) as ballet master, there was a spate of brilliant young dancers, much original choreographic activity and a renewal of Bournonville classics, a happy trend which continues and has had a considerable influence abroad. Several dancers have settled permanently in the U.S.A.: the renowned teacher of the American School of Ballet, Stanley Williams (1925–); Toni Lander (1931–), married to Bruce Marks; and Peter Martins (1946–), star and ballet master-in-chief of the New York City Ballet. Erik Bruhn, in the opinion of most authorities, is the greatest danseur noble of our era, handsome, of elegant physique and a perfectionist in style. Promoted solo dancer at the Royal Danish Ballet, 1949, he also embarked on his international career as guest artist in England, the U.S.A. and Canada, as Director of the Royal Swedish Ballet, 1967–1971, and as artistic director of the National Ballet of Canada, Toronto, July 1983. A versatile, model interpreter of both classic and modern roles, he has also restaged many ballets and is co-author, with Lillian Moore, of *Bournonville and Ballet Technique,* London, 1961. Photo 190 is an action study in *Giselle* with Carla Fracci (ABT, ca. 1972); Photo 191 is ca. 1979. (Photos: Louis Péres)

191

192

193

192. **FLEMMING FLINDT** (1936–) in *Carmen.* Promoted to solo dancer of the Royal Danish Ballet in 1957, Flindt then began to appear as guest artist with the London Festival Ballet, Paris Opéra (as danseur étoile 1961–1964), Ruth Page and Royal Ballets. In 1966, he was named Director of the Royal Danish Ballet. His best-known choreographic work, *The Lesson* (T.V., 1963, and stage version, 1964), has been performed in many countries. (Photo: Mydtskov, Copenhagen) 193. **HENNING KRONSTAM** (1934–) in *Tornerose.* Promoted solo dancer of the Royal Danish Ballet, 1956, Kronstam has had great success in classic, Bournonville and modern ballet and was specially admired both for his dancing and delightful personality when the company visited New York. He was appointed assistant ballet master, 1966, and Director, 1978. (Photo: Mydtskov, Copenhagen)

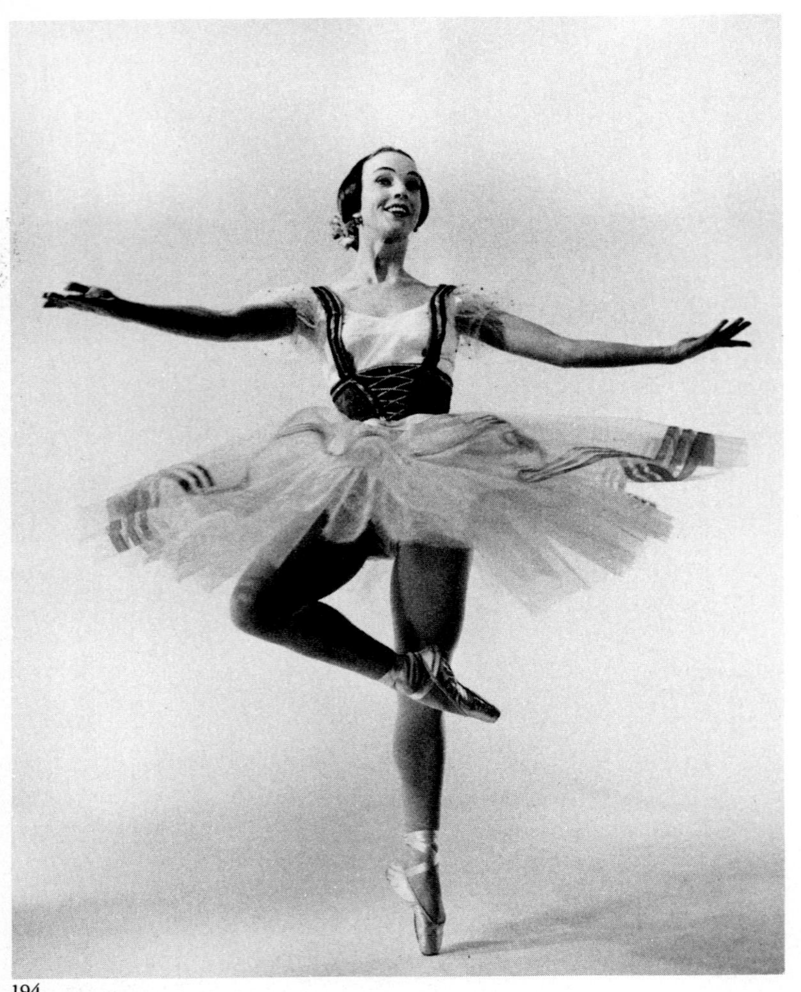

194

194. KIRSTEN RALOV (Kirsten Gnatt, 1922–) in *Napoli.* In 1942 the Royal Danish Ballet promoted her solo dancer, a position she held for 20 years, thereafter remaining with the company as teacher and producer. She has staged Bournonville and other ballets in Denmark, the U.S.A. and elsewhere. (Photo: Mydtskov, Copenhagen) **195 & 196. CARLA FRACCI** (1936–). Idol of the Italian public and of her own devoted following in other countries, Fracci was promoted prima ballerina at La Scala, 1958, and stayed until 1963, returning later as guest artist, while appearing all over Italy, in France, England and with American Ballet Theatre. Although she interprets modern ballets such as Grigorovich's *The Stone Flower* and Butler's *Medea* (Spoleto, 1975; New York, 1976), she is most cherished in Romantic roles, especially *Pas de Quatre* and Giselle, in which she has had as partners nearly all the world-famous premiers danseurs: Bruhn, Kronstam, Nureyev, Bortoluzzi, Vasiliev, Baryshnikov and others. Bruhn called their partnership ideal; Marie Rambert said: "the greatest Giselle of the twentieth century and I have seen them all, including Spessivtseva." Fracci had the role of Karsavina in the film *Nijinsky* (1980) and played Verdi's wife in the Italian television series about the composer, 1983. Married to producer Beppe Menegatti. Photo 195 shows her receiving the medal of Commendatore al Merito della Repubblica; Photo 196 is from 1970. See also Photo 190. (Photo 196: Niki Ekstrom)

195

197

197 & 198. NINI THEILADE (1916–   ). Not to be classified with any national ballet or group, Theilade, born in Java of Danish-Asian parents, first appeared as a child prodigy in Berlin with Max Reinhardt. Since then she has roamed the world, as a concert performer and as a star with the Royal Danish Ballet, with the Ballet Russe de Monte Carlo in New York, where she created a furor in Salvador Dali's *Bacchanale* (1939), and in Brazil, where she resided for nearly 20 years. She has choreographed many ballets, mainly for the Royal Danish Ballet, and, in 1970, opened a school and formed a small company near Svendborg, Denmark. Photo 197 shows her in *Lotosblume,* Berlin, ca. 1928. (Photos: Isabey, Paris)

198

199

199 & 200. MIA SLAVENSKA (Mia Corak, 1914–). Another dancer who cannot be anchored to any country or company, Slavenska, born in Yugoslavia, began her career as prima ballerina of the Zagreb Opera Ballet, followed by appearances in Nijinska's company, Paris, 1933, in Berlin, 1936, in the U.S.A. with Ballet Russe de Monte Carlo, 1938–1942, London Festival Ballet, 1952, Slavenska-Franklin Company, 1952–1955, Metropolitan Opera, 1956, and many others. Golden-haired, beautiful and svelte and trained in the classics by Preobrajenska, Egorova and Kschessinska, she was an exquisite ballerina. After leaving the stage, she settled in California as teacher. In Photo 199 she is in costume for *The Nutcracker;* Photo 200 dates from 1941. (Photo 199: Alfredo Valente)

200

201

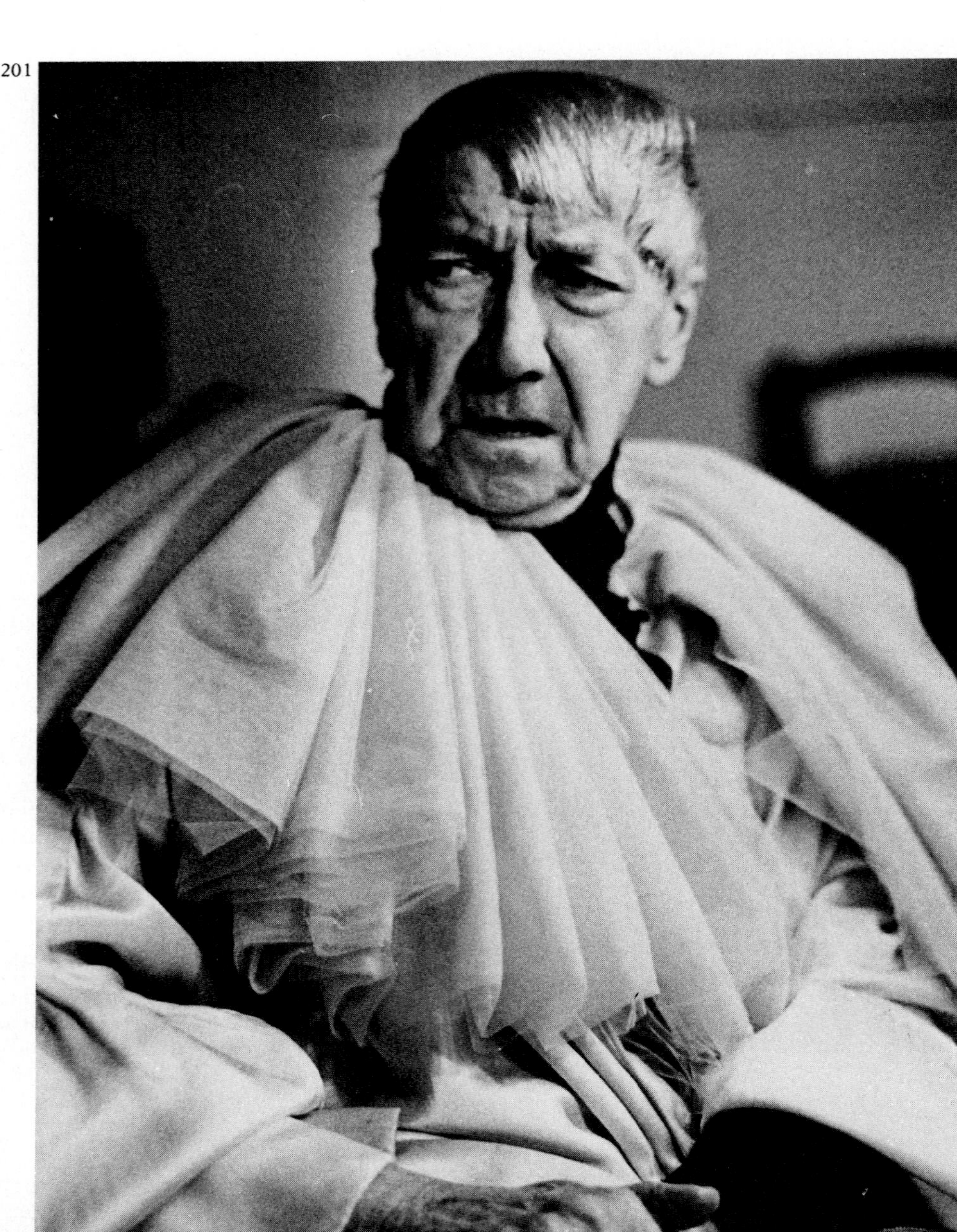

201. EDWARD CATON (1900–1981), last photograph. Caton's peripatetic existence began in St. Petersburg, where his American father was manager of the Czar's stables. Unable, as a foreigner, to enter the Imperial Ballet School, he studied with Nelida and Vaganova. He left Russia with his family at the outbreak of the Revolution and pursued his career on tour with Pavlova; with the Chicago Opera Ballet; the Littlefield Company, Philadelphia; Mordkin Ballet and Ballet Theatre, New York; and Marquis de Cuevas Company, Paris. At various times he held the post of ballet master for the Marquis de Cuevas, Ballet Theatre and Ballet Russe de Monte Carlo, and also taught in France and the U.S.A. His best-known choreography was *Sebastian* (1944), the only ballet that combines music by Menotti and decor by Milena.

202

203

202. VERA ZORINA (Eva Brigitta Hartwig, 1917–   ) in *Persephone* (revival). Zorina's many-faceted career embraces her work in theater, musical comedy, films and ballet and as a *diseuse.* After her debut in Max Reinhardt's *A Midsummer Night's Dream,* she continued as an actress in England and then went to Hollywood to make films. Her outstanding successes were: musical comedy, *On Your Toes* (London, 1937) and Balanchine's *I Married an Angel* (Broadway, 1938); films, *Goldwyn Follies* (1938) and *Star Spangled Rhythm* (1943); ballet, appearances and tours with Ballet Russe de Monte Carlo and Ballet Theatre. She married Balanchine in 1938 and later married Goddard Lieberson, president of Columbia Records. Her stage career continues as a narrator in revivals of the complete Stravinsky-Gide *Persephone,* in which she performed for the Santa Fe Opera, 1962, and as recently as 1982 at Lincoln Center and 1983 on television. She is the author of texts for Columbia Records' album of ballet music and for their *Complete Works of Stravinsky,* 1981. **203. ALEXANDER BENNETT** (1930–   ). A native of Edinburgh, dancer, ballet master, teacher, of great humor and independence, Bennett did not properly begin his ballet career until he was discharged from the army and was taken in hand by Marie Rambert, who recognized his potentialities. Having had no early training, he nevertheless soon became premier danseur of Ballet Rambert in both classic and modern roles. After stints as ballet master of the Transvaal Ballet, 1965, as dancer with Western Theatre Ballet, 1966, and Covent Garden Opera Ballet, 1969, he rejoined the Rambert company. At present he directs the Scottish-America Ballet in Chattanooga and also teaches there at the University of Tennessee, restages ballets there and elsewhere in the U.S.A. and is completing two books, a biography of Dame Marie Rambert and a history of *La Sylphide.*

A series of companies descended from Diaghilev's Ballets Russes, all of them heir to many of his ballets and his dancers. The new enterprises had confusingly similar names—Opéra Russe à Paris (which included ballet); Ballet(s) Russe(s) de Monte Carlo of René Blum (1878–1942) and Colonel W. de Basil (Vassili Voskresensky, 1888–1951), 1932–1935; René Blum's Ballet de Monte Carlo, 1936–1939; Colonel de Basil's Ballet Russe, 1936, which in 1939 became Original Ballet Russe as a result of a law suit with the rival Ballet Russe de Monte Carlo of Sergei Denham (1897–1970), a company which functioned 1938–1962. The Diaghilev dancers, augmented by a new generation, moved back and forth among these organizations to such an extent that it is now impossible to say that any dancer belonged more to one company than to another. The Blum company had a solid base, with Diaghilev's Massine, Balanchine, Woizikowsky and Doubrovska, the great new acquisition being the three much-publicized "baby ballerinas"—Toumanova, Baronova and Riabouchinska—and also David Lichine. **204–206. DAVID LICHINE** (David Liechtenstein, 1910–1972) first appeared with the Ida Rubinstein company, 1928, next with Pavlova, 1930, and then joined Colonel de Basil, with whom he remained until 1941, and then went to the Teatro Colón, Buenos Aires, 1947. A busy and successful choreographer, his most often revived works are the popular *Graduation Ball* (1940) and *La Rencontre, ou Oedipe et le Sphinx* (1948). He married Tatiana Riabouchinska and with her founded a school and the Los Angeles Ballet company. In Photo 205 he appears in *Cotillon* (1932) with Morosova (left) and Baronova. Olga Morosova was the wife of Colonel de Basil and sister of the more famous Nina Verchinina. **IRINA BARONOVA** (1919–   ), "baby ballerina," joined de Basil, 1932, and soon had star roles. Joined Ballet Theatre, 1940, made films and rejoined de Basil, 1946. She married German Sevastianov, business manager of de Basil, divorced him and married Cecil Tennant. After Tennant's death, learning that Sevastianov had cancer, she went to Switzerland and took care of him until his death. In Photo 206 Lichine appears in *Le Bourgeois Gentilhomme* (1932) with **TAMARA TOUMANOVA** (1919–   ). After her debut as a nine-year-old prodigy, Toumanova joined de Basil's company as the third "baby ballerina," then Balanchine's Les Ballets 1933, followed by four more years with de Basil, during which she created many important roles, then Original Ballet Russe, 1939, and Denham's Ballet Russe, 1941. She has been seen in musical comedy and many films and as a star guest performer here and abroad. As slim and raven-haired as Baronova was curvaceous and blonde, Toumanova remains in memory as one of the most beautiful ballerinas of our era; see also Photo 99.

204

205

206

208

207 & 208. The name of **TATIANA RIABOUCHINSKA** (1917–   ) can be properly associated with Colonel de Basil's Ballet Russe for, after her debut with the Chauve-Souris revue, she was engaged with the other two "baby ballerinas," 1932, and she continued to appear with de Basil for ten years in Europe, the U.S.A. and Australia. No one who saw it could ever forget her electrifying performance, her flights across the stage and astounding elevation as the Golden Cockerel (Photo 207, Fokine revival, 1937) nor her innocent charm as the schoolgirl in *Graduation Ball* (1940). Later she was a glittering guest ballerina in America, Paris and London, and at present is teaching at the Los Angeles school which she founded with her late husband, David Lichine. Photo 208 shows her in *Cendrillon* (1938). (Photo 207: Gordon Anthony, London)

209

209 & 210. YUREK SHABELEVSKY (1911–   ) joined de Basil's company, 1932, after studies in Warsaw and with Nijinska and some appearances with Ida Rubinstein. During his seven years with de Basil, this handsome Polish dancer excelled in character roles and in revivals such as *Petrouchka* and *Schéhérazade*. After further international engagements as guest artist, he was appointed ballet master of the New Zealand Ballet, 1967. Photo 210 shows him in *Polovtsian Dances from Prince Igor,* revival. (Photo 210: Mme. S. Georges, London)

210

211

212

211. TAMARA GRIGORIEVA (Tamara Sidorenko, 1918–) in *L'Après-midi d'un faune,* revival (with David Lichine), 1936. Exceptionally beautiful, flaxen-haired, slender and tall, Grigorieva made her debut in Balanchine's Les Ballets 1933, but a few months later joined de Basil, remaining with him until 1944 and starring in most of the Diaghilev revivals as well as the new works. Subsequently she was guest artist and ballet mistress in Rio de Janeiro, Montevideo and Buenos Aires. **212. ROMAN JASINSKI** (Roman Czeslaw, 1912–). By the time he was 21, this remarkable Polish classic dancer had appeared with Ida Rubinstein, with Lifar in concert performances and with Massine at La Scala, and had joined de Basil. After brief absences for Les Ballets 1933 and some U.S.A. appearances with Lifar, he returned to de Basil as a permanent premier danseur for 14 years. Later he toured with Markova, with Toumanova and with Danilova. He married Moscelyne Larkin (1925–), an American dancer, known during her de Basil days as Moussia Larkina, and together they set up a school in Tulsa, where they founded and now direct the Tulsa Civic Ballet, a splendid undertaking for which Jasinski also choreographs new works and stages revivals. (Photo: Ermates-Mahardze, N.Y.)

213

214

213. IRINA BOROWSKA (1930–), an Argentine-born dancer, began her career with the Teatro Colón. In 1954, she joined Denham's Ballet Russe de Monte Carlo, remaining for five years, and then had guest appearances with Chicago Opera Ballet and London Festival Ballet. In 1966, she married Karl Musil, premier danseur of the Vienna Staatsoper, and she now teaches in Vienna. (Photo: Saul Goodman) **214. MIKHAIL KATCHAROFF** (1913–) as the Dandy in *Le Tricorne,* revival. Danced with Opéra Russe à Paris, 1930, and Ida Rubinstein, 1931, and the following year joined de Basil. He was ballet master for both de Basil and Denham's Ballet Russe, meanwhile performing delightfully in many revival roles such as Coppelius in *Coppélia* and the Chief Eunuch in *Schéhérazade.* Born in Persia, his career has taken him all over the world and he is now settled in New York. (Photo: Maurice Seymour, Chicago)

215

215. **ANDRÉ EGLEVSKY** (1917–1977). Noblest of the danseurs nobles, Eglevsky was only 14 when he joined de Basil, but he had acquired such a controlled and brilliant technique from studying with Egorova, Kschessinska, Volinine and Legat that almost immediately he was cast in leading roles. During a 41-year career with de Basil, René Blum, Denham, the Marquis de Cuevas company and (the final seven years) the New York City Ballet, he created important roles for Massine and Balanchine and was an ideal interpreter of the classics, always astounding in his slow, controlled pirouettes, his elevation and even his very personal walk on stage. Fokine said: "Eglevsky can do anything Nijinsky could." He was filmed, 1952, in Charlie Chaplin's *Limelight* and on television's Kate Smith show. In 1958 with his wife, Leda Anchutina, he opened a school on Long Island, New York, formed a small but successful company and taught, numbering among his accomplished pupils his daughter Marina (1951–). Co-author with John Gregory of *The Heritage of a Ballet Master: Nicolas Legat,* New York, 1977. (Photo: Serge Lido)

216

217

216 & 217. LEON DANIELIAN (1920–). One of the rare New Yorkers to become an outstanding, internationally known premier danseur, Danielian made his debut with the Mordkin Ballet, 1937, and since then his peregrinations have taken him to the four corners of the world—Europe, North and South America, North Africa, the Middle East and Asia, with Ballet Theatre, de Basil, Ballets des Champs-Elysées, on tour with Chauviré, the San Francisco Ballet, not to mention an eight-year period with Denham's Ballet Russe de Monte Carlo. His wide range embraced everything from bravura roles in the classics to comedy and character roles. He has choreographed a number of ballets, was appointed director of the American Ballet Theatre School, 1968, and at present teaches in Texas. Photo 216 shows him in *Don Quixote* (1955); Photo 217, in 1981. (Photo 216: Constantine; Photo 217: Ken Duncan, N.Y.)

218. Mary Ellen Moylan and Nicholas Magallanes in *Ballet Imperial,* revival. The all too brief career of **MARY ELLEN MOYLAN** (1926–) began when she was 16 and ended at 31, when she opted for marriage rather than the stage. Her two major engagements were with Ballet Russe de Monte Carlo, 1943–1944 and 1947–1949, and with American Ballet Theatre, 1949–1955, followed by musical comedy and television shows. **NICHOLAS MAGALLANES** (1922–1977) was a Mexican-born dancer who first performed with Ballet Caravan, 1941, then with Littlefield Ballet, 1942, and Ballet Russe de Monte Carlo, 1943–1946. His name, however, will always be identified with the New York City Ballet, where he was premier danseur for 27 long years, perennially youthful. His courtly manners, both as performer and in private life, endeared him to everyone. See also Photo 235. (Photo: Maurice Seymour, Chicago)

219

219. FREDERIC FRANKLIN (1941–). Born in Liverpool, Franklin first emerged in revues and musical shows, sang and danced with Mistinguett, 1931, and after four more years of this kind, embarked on serious ballet with the Markova-Dolin company. In 1938, he joined the Ballet Russe and immediately established himself as a dancer of fine technical ability, great verve and personal charm. A few highlights from his extraordinarily active career include: Covent Garden, in his already celebrated partnership with Danilova, 1949; tour of the U.S.A., Hawaii, the Philippines and Japan with the Slavenska-Franklin company, 1951; renewed engagement with Ballet Russe, as ballet master and premier danseur, 1954–1956; tour in South Africa with Danilova; director-choreographer of National Ballet of Washington, D.C., 1956–1960. Endowed with a remarkable memory, he has restaged and choreographed many ballets for many companies, an activity that still absorbs him and can be seen in the film he made with Danilova, *Reflections of a Dancer,* 1981. The following year he celebrated his fiftieth anniversary on the stage. (Photo: Alfredo Valente)

220. NATHALIE KRASSOVSKA (Natasha Leslie, 1919–) in *Le Bourgeois Gentilhomme* (1944). A third-generation Russian dancer, Krassovska set out on her road to fame with Nijinska's company, 1932, and Les Ballets 1933. She was with the Ballet Russe de Monte Carlo, 1936–1950, applauded as a very pretty, graceful, accomplished dancer, and after that long stint was with London Festival Ballet, 1950–1955. Later she was guest artist with the Ballet Russe, Festival Ballet, Ballet Rambert, Marquis de Cuevas and other companies, but since the mid-sixties has been in semiretirement in Texas. (Photo: Maurice Seymour, Chicago)

221

221. LUCIA CHASE (1907–) as the Queen in *Bluebeard,* 1941, with Enrique Martinez (left) and Jerome Robbins (see Photo 233). Lucia Chase studied with Vilzak, Nijinska and other notable teachers including Mikhail Mordkin, in whose company she danced, 1939–1940. In 1940, she founded Ballet Theatre (later American Ballet Theatre) together with Richard Pleasant (1906–1961), former manager for Mordkin, and Oliver Smith (1918–), an artist who designed many productions for the new company: *Rodeo, Fall River Legend, Fancy Free* and others. Under the aegis of Lucia Chase, who also invested much of her personal fortune, American Ballet Theatre became one of the two leading companies in the U.S.A., bringing many important foreign choreographers and dancers to this country while always placing great emphasis on American talent. Meanwhile, Lucia Chase continued appearing as a performer. In 1981 she retired and the reins were handed over to Mikhail Baryshnikov. **ENRIQUE MARTINEZ** (1926–), a pupil of Alicia Alonso and Igor Schwezoff (1904–1982), joined American Ballet Theatre in 1940, was promoted soloist four years later and eventually became ballet master. (Photo: Oleaga) 222. Antony Tudor and Eugene Loring in *The Great American Goof* (1940). One of the U.S.A.'s greatest ballet acquisitions was **ANTONY TUDOR,** who arrived for Ballet Theatre's first season with his friend Hugh Laing and a portfolio of the ballets he had choreographed in London for Marie Rambert, the Vic-Wells and his own London Ballet. Tudor had limitations as a dancer, having begun to study only as a grown man, but his ballets were very new and original, mainly "psychological" ballets that depended as much on the dancers' dramatic abilities as on their technical prowess. For Ballet Theatre he restaged his *Lilac Garden (Jardin aux Lilas), Gala Performance, Judgment of Paris* and *Dark Elegies* and then created a series of masterpieces, including *Pillar of Fire* (1942), *Romeo and Juliet* (1943) and *Dim Lustre* (1943). After 1950, he was director of the Metropolitan Opera Ballet School, headed the dance department at the Juilliard School and for the year 1963 was artistic director of the Royal Swedish Ballet. At present, very involved with Indian philosophy and meditation, he emerges occasionally as guest choreographer and is also adviser to, and a director of, American Ballet Theatre. **EUGENE LORING** (1914–1982) studied at the School of American Ballet, 1936. He created *The Great American Goof* for the opening of the new Ballet Theatre and continued choreographing many ballets for stage and films. He established a school in Los Angeles and finally joined the faculty of the University of California. (Photo: Gjon Mili)

222

224

223

223. NORA KAYE (Nora Koreff, 1920–) in *Pillar of Fire* (1942). Although trained as a classical ballerina, Nora Kaye reached the supreme heights of her career in the dramatic roles of Tudor's ballets and has never been equaled. She first danced with Metropolitan Opera Ballet and at Radio City Music Hall, then joined Ballet Theatre and, except for a three-year absence with New York City Ballet, 1951–1954, has remained with that company for some 20 years and is now one of its directors. Married to Herbert Ross (1926–), she collaborated with him in founding the Festival of Two Worlds, Spoleto, 1960, and in producing musical comedies and films, especially *Nijinsky* (1980). See also Photo 225. (Photo: Alfredo Valente) **224. SALLIE WILSON** (1932–). Although she is a distinguished interpreter of classic ballet, Sallie Wilson achieved great personal triumphs in Tudor's dramatic roles. At 17, she joined Ballet Theatre and stayed with that company except for some appearances with Metropolitan Opera Ballet, 1950–1955, and a brief association with New York City Ballet. In addition to guest engagements, she is now embarked on a new career as choreographer. (Photo: Maurice Seymour, N.Y.)

225

226

225. HUGH LAING (Hugh Skinner, 1911–) with Nora Kaye in *Romeo and Juliet*. Laing, a strikingly handsome, dramatic performer, was long associated with Tudor, who choreographed many roles for him in Marie Rambert's company, Tudor's London Ballet, at Ballet Theatre from its inception and at New York City Ballet, 1951–1952. Upon retiring, he became a professional photographer, established in New York. See also Photo 142. (Photo: Gjon Mili) **226.** Alicia Alonso and Igor Youskevitch in the *Nutcracker* pas de deux (1946). **ALICIA ALONSO** (Alicia Ernestina Martínez, 1917–), the celebrated Cuban dancer, emerged in the U.S.A. in Broadway musicals and Ballet Caravan. She was with Ballet Theatre for nearly 20 years, 1941–1960, during which time she and Youskevitch achieved their extraordinary partnership. During absences from Ballet Theatre, she danced in Cuba and founded her own Ballet Alicia Alonso, eventually the Ballet de Cuba, and also appeared with Ballet Russe de Monte Carlo. A serious eye affliction caused her to become nearly blind, but now, almost cured by surgery, she still dances occasionally as a guest star or at galas. **IGOR YOUSKEVITCH** (1912–). Like Tudor, Youskevitch did not begin ballet until he was 20, but his background as an athlete hastened his progress so that two years later he danced with Nijinska's company and then in rapid succession with Woizikowsky, 1935, de Basil, 1937, and Ballet Russe de Monte Carlo, 1938–1943. By the time he joined Ballet Theatre, 1946–1955, he was one of the most eminent danseurs of our era. He established a school on Long Island, N.Y., then directed the dance department at the University of Texas, Austin, and after ten years there, retired, 1982, at a gala attended by 3000 admiring Texans and hundreds of visiting ballet celebrities. (Photo: Gjon Mili)

227

227 & 228. AGNES DE MILLE (1909–). More celebrated as choreographer and author than as dancer, she nevertheless performed with Marie Rambert's company and in European and American recitals. She choreographed, among other ballets, for Ballet Theatre the witty *Three Virgins and a Devil* (1941) and the dour, dramatic *Fall River Legend* (1948) and for Ballet Russe de Monte Carlo her novel and superlative *Rodeo,* 1942. De Mille has had enormous success as an innovator in musical comedies such as *Oklahoma!* and *One Touch of Venus* (1943), *Bloomer Girl* (1944), *Carousel* (1945), *Brigadoon* (1947) and *Gentlemen Prefer Blondes* (1949), as well as in films, television and on the lecture platform. She has worked tirelessly in official circles to better conditions for dancers and is a prolific author: *Dance to the Piper* (1951), *And Promenade Home* (1958), *The Book of the Dance* (1963), *Speak to Me, Dance with Me* (1973), *America Dances* (1980). Photo 227 shows her in *Elizabethan Suite* (London, 1938); Photo 228, in 1982. (Photo 227: Angus MacBean, London; Photo 228: Jack Mitchell)

229

229. MARIA KARNILOVA (1920–   ) in *Three Virgins and a Devil* (1941). After an early debut with the Metropolitan Opera Children's Ballet, Karnilova appeared briefly with various companies and joined the newly formed Ballet Theatre, 1939–1948. She is now mainly known for musical comedy, especially *Gypsy* (1959) and *Fiddler on the Roof* (1964), for which she received a Tony Award. She was given a great welcome when she danced in American Ballet Theatre's 35th Anniversary Gala, 1975. (Photo: Semo, Mexico City) **230 & 231. GEORGE SKIBINE** (1920–1981). Skibine's first stage appearance was at age five, in the fair scene of Diaghilev's *Petrouchka*. In 1938, he was a member of Blum's Ballet de Monte Carlo, joined de Basil, 1941, Ballet Theatre, 1941–1942, Markova-Dolin company, 1947. That year he married Marjorie Tallchief and established their celebrated partnership. They appeared together with the Marquis de Cuevas Company, 1947–1956, and were danseurs étoiles at the Paris Opéra, where Skibine was also ballet master, 1958–1962. After a short stint with the Lübeck Opera, Skibine was artistic director of the Harkness Ballet, New York, 1964–1966, and, finally, director of the Dallas Ballet Academy, Texas. A dancer of great refinement and charm, he was also a very active choreographer. Photo 230 shows him in 1946; Photo 231, with Marjorie Tallchief in *Annabel Lee* (1951). The career of **MARJORIE TALLCHIEF** (1927–   ) has largely paralleled her husband's. When she was engaged by the Paris Opéra, with Skibine, she was the first American ever to be given the rank of danseuse étoile by that august institution. After her husband's premature death, she continued to run the Dallas Academy and now is settled in Chicago with the school and company of her sister, Maria Tallchief.

230

231

232

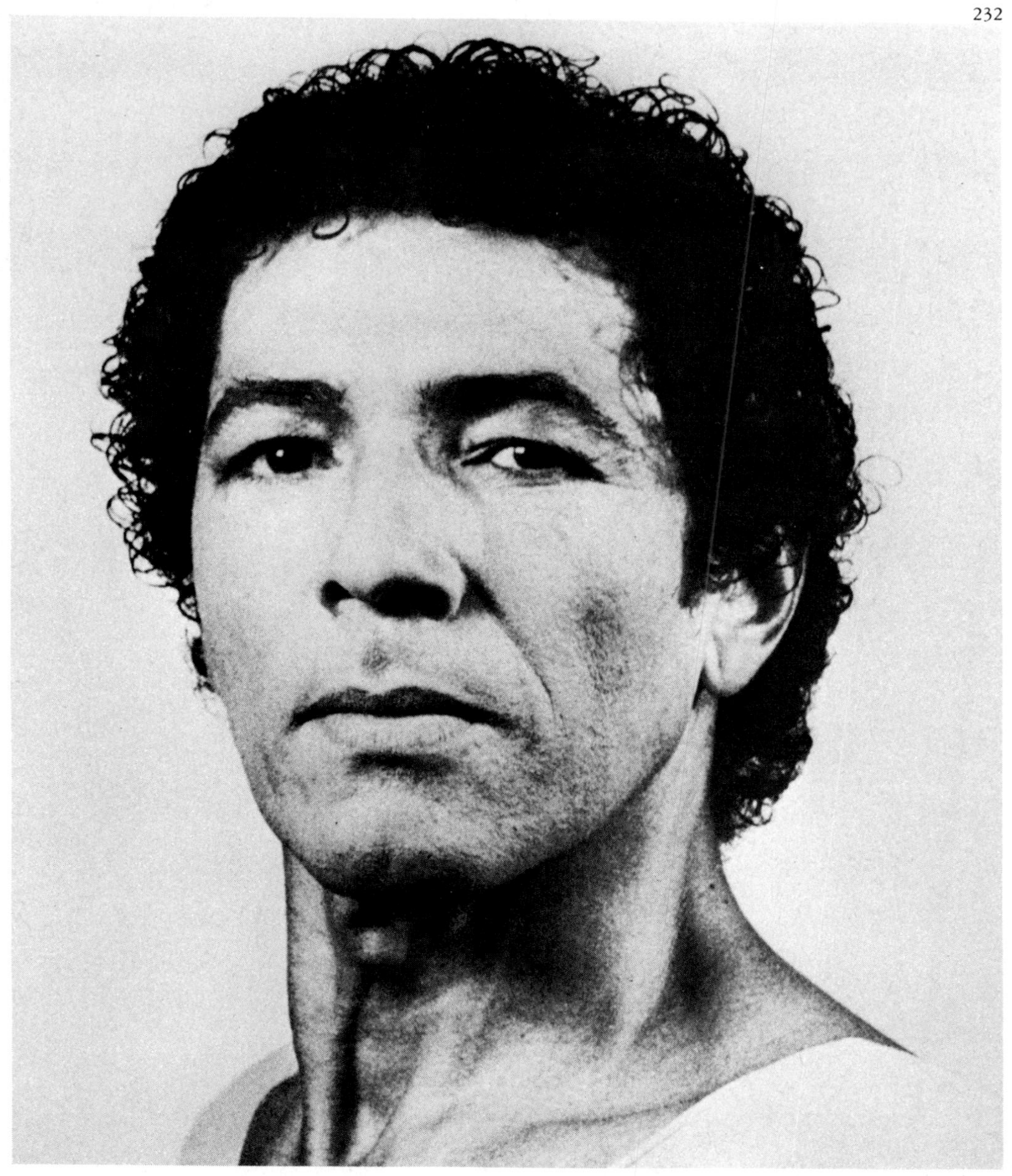

232. FRANCISCO MONCION (1922–   ). Moncion studied at the School of American Ballet and first attracted attention dancing the lead in *Sebastian,* 1944, produced by Ballet International (later Grand Ballet du Marquis de Cuevas) with choreography by Edward Caton, music by Gian-Carlo Menotti and decor and costumes by Milena. In 1946, Moncion joined Balanchine's and Kirstein's Ballet Society, remained with them when they established the New York City Ballet and is still an admired member of that company. Although his schooling and a 35-year career were under the aegis of Balanchine, he has a very distinct personality of his own. When not performing, he is a "Sunday painter." (Photo: Ted Leyson, 1975)

233

234

235

233. **JEROME ROBBINS** (J. Rabinowitz, 1918–) in *Capriccio Espagnol,* revival. Robbins, with extraordinary results, has explored every aspect of stage production and dance—musical comedy, straight theater, films, television, classic ballet and jazz—and is today the outstanding American choreographer. He first danced in musical comedy and when he joined Ballet Theatre, 1940, his roles ranged from classical to character and comedy. He performed with New York City Ballet, 1949, and was associate artistic director, 1950–1959. He founded and choreographed for his own touring company, Ballets: U.S.A., 1958, rejoined New York City Ballet, 1968, and is now, with Peter Martins, ballet master-in-chief there. A partial list of his works must include his popular, often-revived *Fancy Free,* for Ballet Theatre (1944); for his first period with New York City Ballet, *The Cage* and *The Pied Piper* (1951) and *The Afternoon of a Faun* (1953); for American Ballet Theatre, a new and powerful version of *Les Noces;* and for his second New York City Ballet period and present affiliation, the pure poetry of *Dances at a Gathering* (1969) and *The Goldberg Variations* (1971). Of Robbins' many works for theater most notable are *West Side Story* (1957), a milestone in the development of the musical, and *Fiddler on the Roof* (1964), both later made into films. Should one hesitate to apply the word genius to this life work? See also Photo 221. (Photo: Alfredo Valente) 234. **MARIA TALLCHIEF** (1925–). It is a fascinating thought that, all at once, Oklahoma produced five ballerinas, all of them American Indian and all of them of great international repute—the glamorous Maria Tallchief and her sister Marjorie, Rosella Hightower (see Photo 101), Moscelyne Larkin and Yvonne Chouteau (1929–). Maria Tallchief's first major engagements were with the Ballet Russe de Monte Carlo, 1942–1947 and 1954–1955, and she next became the brightest star in the firmament of the New York City Ballet, 1947–1960 and 1963–1965. With her diamantine technical glitter (quite the opposite of her sister Marjorie's poetic lyricism), she gave dazzling performances in classical ballet and especially in the works of Balanchine (to whom she was married, 1946–1952), her interpretation of his *Firebird* being unforgettable. As a guest star, she was seen with Paris Opéra, 1947, and Chicago Opera Ballet and Chicago Lyric Opera, 1961–1962, and was awarded a prize at the International Festival, Paris. At present, she directs a company and a school in Chicago. (Photo: Maurice Seymour, Chicago) 235. **VIOLETTE VERDY** (Nelly Guillerm, 1933–) and Nicholas Magallanes in *Swan Lake.* As a mere child, Verdy appeared with the Ballets des Champs-Elysées; then, after meandering from one company to another, she reached the summit of her career as ballerina of the New York City Ballet, 1958–1972, very popular and much admired for her Gallic vivacity and meticulous technique in a wide variety of roles. She was appointed director of ballet at the Paris Opéra, 1977, then co-director of the Boston Ballet, a post she resigned in 1984. She is now back in the fold of the New York City Ballet. (Photo: William Vasillov, 1961)

236

236–238. **TANAQUIL LE CLERCQ** (1929–). The world of ballet mourned when "Tanny's" dancing career was tragically ended by her contracting polio in Denmark, 1956, while on tour with the New York City Ballet. Entirely the product of one organization, she studied with the School of American Ballet before joining Ballet Society/New York City Ballet, 1946–1956. Her willowy figure and incredibly long, slim legs gave a very personal quality to her dancing; she was adored by the public, who will not forget the roles she created for Balanchine (to whom she was married, 1952–1969) and for Jerome Robbins, in whose *Afternoon of a Faun* she was irreplaceable. After a period of readjustment following her illness, she wrote two books, *Mourka: The Autobiography of a Cat* (1964) and *The Ballet Cookbook* (1967), and embarked as a teacher at the school connected with the Dance Theatre of Harlem. Photo 236 shows her in *Western Symphony* (1954); Photo 237, in *Metamorphoses* (1952); and Photo 238, in *Illuminations* (1950). (Photos: George Platt Lynes, N.Y.)

237

238

239

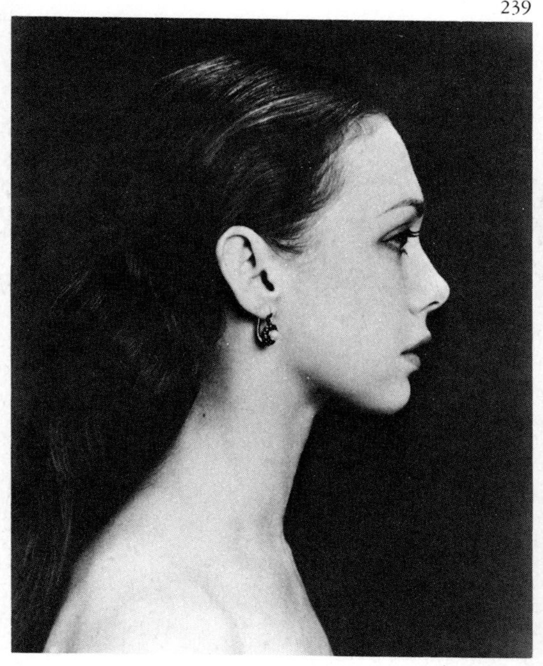

240

239 & 240. ALLEGRA KENT (1938–) first appeared with New York City Ballet, 1953, and was promoted ballerina, 1957, starring in classical, Balanchine and Robbins roles. Particularly memorable was her ethereal rendition of the Sleepwalker in *Night Shadow,* the revival of *La Somnambule* (Photo 240). She has been seen on television and returns occasionally to perform for the New York City Ballet and as a guest star at galas. She also teaches in New York and elsewhere and is the author of *Joseph Cornell: A Reminiscence* (Joseph Cornell Portfolio) and *Allegra Kent's Water Beauty Book* (1976). See also Photo 242. (Photos: Martha Swope)

241

241 & 242. EDWARD VILLELLA (1937–). Villella's many-faceted career began with the School of American Ballet, and from 1957 he was one of the outstanding members of the New York City Ballet. A dancer endowed with technique, plasticity and dramatic power, he was especially memorable in Balanchine's *The Prodigal Son.* He has appeared in musicals and films and on television and has choreographed. In 1978 he was appointed by Mayor Koch as Commissioner of Cultural Affairs, and in 1982, he was named Producer-Director of PBS' "Dance in America" series and the same year became Director-Advisor of the Eglevsky Company and School. A natural gift for public speaking and an irresistible smile have added greatly to his popularity. Villella has now resigned from his positions with "Dance in America" and the Eglevsky Company, and was named artistic director of Ballet Oklahoma for 1983–1984. In Photo 242 he is seen with Allegra Kent in *Bugaku* (1963). (Photo 241: Don Perdue, 1982; Photo 242: Bert Stern)

242

243

243. JACQUES D'AMBOISE (1934–). After studying at the School of American Ballet, d'Amboise joined the New York City Ballet and three years later was promoted soloist. Although he began as a rather overweight, all-American athletic type, he soon developed into a lean, sinuous classical dancer and, for 30 years, was a loved and respected star of the company, for which he created many Balanchine roles and also choreographed several ballets. (Photo: Chris Alexander, 1975)

244

245

244 & 245. We are told that **JOHN TARAS** (1919–) first danced in public when he was nine and choreographed his first ballet at the age of 13. One might add that he has never stopped since then, and the mere thought of his ceaseless activity is breathtaking. He has danced with American Ballet Caravan, 1940; Littlefield Company, 1941; Ballet Theatre, 1942–1946; de Basil, the Marquis de Cuevas and New York City Ballet; he has been ballet master for all of these companies except for the first two and was also appointed ballet master at the Paris Opéra, 1969–1970. He has choreographed and staged for Ballet Theatre, Markova-Dolin company, de Basil, Ballet Society, the Metropolitan and the San Francisco Ballets, Marquis de Cuevas, Teatro Colón, National Ballet of Chile, Netherlands Ballet, the Monte Carlo Opera (for the marriage of Prince Rainier), Royal Danish, Dance Theatre of Harlem and many others, but mainly with the New York City Ballet. From 1959, he was one of the triumvirate of ballet masters (with Balanchine and Robbins) directing the New York City Ballet, where he produced his *Ebony Concerto* (1960) and various new works for the two Stravinsky festivals. His *Designs for Strings* is often revived. In 1984 he resigned from his position with the New York City Ballet and became Associate Director with Mikhail Baryshnikov of American Ballet Theatre. In Photo 244, the man at the right in the scene from a *Billy the Kid* revival is Alpheus Koon (1918–1969), who was with Ballet Theatre before joining Original Ballet Russe, 1946–1947. Photo 245 dates from the early 1980s. (Photo 244: Fred Fehl, N.Y.; Photo 245: Arthur Elgort)

246

247

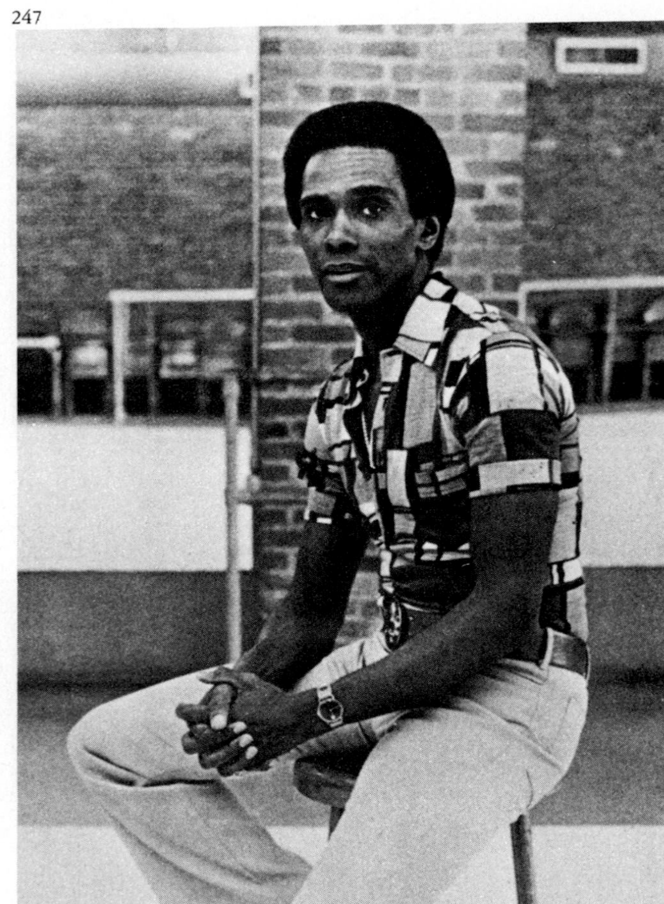

246. KAREL SHOOK (1920–). Two separate careers merged to found the Dance Theatre of Harlem. Karel Shook had danced with the Seattle Civic Opera Ballet, with Ballet Russe de Monte Carlo and in musical comedy, but his special background for the Harlem venture was as director of ballet at the Katherine Dunham School and running his own New York school, 1954–1957, and as ballet master at the J. Taylor School. He also taught and was ballet master for the Dutch National Ballet, 1959. In 1968, he formed a partnership with Arthur Mitchell, starting a school in the basement of a Harlem church and, by 1971, the Dance Theatre of Harlem was a functioning company. The first all-black company with a classical program, as well as interesting revivals and new works, it now has a fine reputation in the U.S.A. and Europe, and the school, now housed in its own building, has a curriculum that includes not only ballet, but costume making and design and music. Karel Shook is the author of *Elements of Classical Ballet Technique* (1977). **247. ARTHUR MITCHELL** (1934–) appeared on Broadway and with the McKayle and Butler companies before joining the New York City Ballet, 1956. There he fulfilled his career as an extremely gifted and popular premier danseur, especially admired in *Ebony Concerto* (1960) and *Agon* (1967). Since founding the Dance Theatre of Harlem with Karel Shook, he has trained many accomplished dancers, handing on to them the benefits of his long experience with Balanchine and presenting them in his excellent revivals of *Agon* and of Bronislava Nijinska's *Les Biches,* as well as the new works he has choreographed for them. In addition to being proud of his company's great success, Mitchell likes to dwell on the asset that the school is to the neighborhood and its underprivileged youth. "Of course, not all of them will become dancers," he says, "but they are learning to appreciate ballet, art and music. They enjoy it and it keeps them off the streets." (Photo: Allen Green) **248. RON SEQUOIO** (1937–) in *La Traviata,* Metropolitan Opera Ballet, 1959. Sequoio began his career in Australia with the company of Edward Boronovsky (1902–1959) and then appeared with Ballet Theatre and the Metropolitan Opera Ballet. He was founder, director, choreographer and dancer with Manhattan Festival Ballet, 1965–1967, then director of dance, Santa Fe Opera, 1966–1969, and artistic director, Kansas City Ballet, 1978–1979. His choreography includes ballets created and restaged for the London Festival Ballet, Danish and Norwegian television, American Ballet Theatre Workshop, Santa Fe Opera, New York City Opera, Manhattan Festival Ballet and others. In many of his ventures he has been associated with James de Bolt (1940–), dancer-soloist with the Joffrey, New York City and Manhattan Festival Ballets, the Norwegian National Ballet and others; choreographer, teacher and designer of decors and costumes. (Photo: Marcus Blackman)

248